VALLEY
OF THE
AMAZONS

Also by Noretta Koertge:
Who Was That Masked Woman?

VALLEY
OF THE
AMAZONS

NORETTA KOERTGE

St. Martin's Press
New York

Design by Manuela Paul

Library of Congress Cataloging in Publication Data

Koertge, Noretta.
    Valley of the amazons.

    I. Title.
PS3561.0345V3   1984   813'.54   83–24683
ISBN 0–312–83608–2

First Edition
10 9 8 7 6 5 4 3 2 1

I hope that this book of traveler's tales may serve as a guide book for gay people, both women and men, who are puzzled and intrigued by contemporary lesbian-feminist culture. It is neither comprehensive, nor up-to-date. Things are changing far too rapidly for that; besides, California will never be quite like the Midwest. My account is critical at times, but it is written with great affection.

Dedicated to the womyn and gay men in Booneville, U.S.A.

Noretta Koertge

Contents

VALLEY
OF THE
AMAZONS

1.

Gay Community Noose

"Hey, Murph! I'm back." Three hairy Hoosier hounds wiggled their welcome.

"Let's see your haircut. Great Goddess, Tretona, why do you always let TJ skin you? Especially in the winter I'd think you'd want a few curls over your ears."

Tretona negotiated the doggie gauntlet and sank into a chair. "Listen to this: TJ came out to me today."

"What do you mean, *came out?* TJ is the faggiest hairdresser in town, and he's always cruising like crazy down at Bullwinkles. If he came out any further, he'd be out of his drawers."

"What I mean is, he came out as a Christian!"

"TJ?"

Tretona felt a tinge of up-manship. (Up-personship? Better give that a feminist analysis, she thought.) It wasn't very often that she knew gossip about the gay community before Helen Murphy did.

"During the shampoo, I noticed he wasn't talking much. You know how he's generally at his bitchy best when he's got you down and lathered up. When we were back at the mirror I noticed that his shirt was buttoned up, and then I saw the cross on his little golden chain."

"Jee-sus!" Helen reverted to patriarchal swearing when she was really upset. "What on earth did you say?"

"Well, I didn't say anything. He saw me looking at the crucifix though. At first I thought it was just some new craze—

1

you know, gold razor blades, earrings, swastikas, who can keep up! But then TJ got real serious, said he had something important to tell me, hoped we could still be friends, didn't expect me to agree . . . but."

"You weren't kidding about it being a coming-out scene! Whatever got into TJ? Or should I say *who* got into him. I hear that new Unitarian minister swings both ways."

Tretona sighed. "Unfortunately no, it's some real Christian outfit got ahold of him. He's singing for Sunday evening services. He's moving into a co-op house they run. He even took a girl to the movies." Tretona waited for Murph to castigate her. Any female over eleven was a *woman*—correction: womyn.

But Helen pushed for details. "What happened? Did he fall in love with the preacher or a choir boy or . . . ?"

Tretona hesitated. Helen wasn't going to like the answer. "I guess he got kind of fed up with the gay community—he went through quite a litany—you know the stuff about meat markets, people always bed hopping, skimming and rimming. And I don't think he ever did get over Dennis. He also said something about his sister having cancer."

Tretona was glad that Helen took off on the cancer tangent. Helen would be the last person ever to admit that there was something seriously wrong with the gay community—well, at least with the feminist branch of it. Helen was anti-monogamy and thought jealousy feelings were a hangover from patriarchal ideas about possessing womyn and children. Helen was pro promiscuity and sexual diversity. "There's no better way to bond sisters together than through mutual pleasuring," she was always saying.

For the sake of argument, Tretona would sometimes ask, "What about bonding brothers and sisters together?" but Helen had a long analysis of why androgyny was a good thing but bisexuality was a cop-out that Tretona never did quite follow.

Boy, TJ had sounded burnt-out when he talked about the gay community. "It's all so superficial. They all act like getting a good lay was the only important thing in life. Since I found

Jesus I've realized it's really the least important—unless you want to have children."

Under Tretona's questioning it soon transpired that the minister had given him the old routine about how he couldn't help being a homosexual—maybe God even made him that way. But he *could* help acting on his unnatural impulses.

Helen was still agitated. "What did you do, Tretona? Didn't you try to talk him out of it?"

Tretona phrased her reply carefully, hoping not to provoke an argument. "Well, I said there were gay Christian alternatives. I told him about the Dignity meetings on Thursday night over at the rectory."

What she hadn't mentioned to TJ and wouldn't discuss with Helen was the undignified atmosphere at those meetings. Father McCawley always drank too much wine and after the book report and formal discussion period he would turn raunchy and start talking about how he'd been down on his knees all night long.

"Were you praying, Father," "someone would shout.

"No, but I sure had my mouth open," would come the reply.

Poor TJ wouldn't find much moral uplift there. The Metropolitan Community Church group down in Cincinnati was supposed to be better, but it was too far to drive, especially if you hoped to meet somebody that way.

Helen took off for a meeting of the bookstore collective, taking the dogs with her, so Tretona was left alone with her ambivalence. Why had she gotten so negative and disillusioned about the whole gay scene? It was only a little over three years ago that she had been so high—the first gay coffee shop had just opened and they'd won their case when the city tried to close them down on some phony excuse about fire regulations. Plus she'd come out in a lecture on Lesbianism to Dr. Williams' Human Sexuality class, and she'd just met Teresa. Ah yes, terrible Teresa, the Olympic-class two-timer. Maybe that was when it turned sour. But it wasn't fair to blame the whole community for that. What *had* gone wrong? And what could be done about it?

Tretona made herself a cup of Red Zinger and headed for the bedroom. There was Zelda the cockatiel perched as usual on the light above the marijuana plants. Helen, who was entering a chemically free phase, had threatened to dispose of them, but so far Tretona had been successful with a right-to-life pitch, using other rhetoric, of course. Tretona took a note pad from the table, drew up three columns, and started to scribble: What I Wanted, What I Got, and What I Can Do About It. Zelda left her warm light fixture and scratched around companionably in the feed tray.

2.

"We Are Fam-i-ly!"

Autumn was Booneville's best season, but Tretona always hated to see the summer end. Summer meant theatre in London, crêpes at the Asterix on King's Road, nude sunbathing at the Women's Pond (where, given the English weather, goosebumps outnumbered freckles, but still).

In London, you need never be far from the gay community —you could always go to a gay pub before the theatre. Half the café types on the King's Road were reading the *Gay News*. Even the regular newspapers were full of juicy stories about Jeremy Thorpe or some judge who got off on slapping the bottoms of the sailor boys hired to run his yacht.

And then there was the weekly ritual—start off with Sunday brunch at the Gates to get the latest dirt. Tuesday night at Sappho's—you could hear everything from Hepzibah Menuhin on the evils of clitorectomies in Africa to the latest direct actions taken by LAIR (Lesbians for Animals' Irreducible Rights). The discussion would be fierce, worthy of Speaker's Corner in Hyde Park, with Nigerian medical students shouting about the provincialism of British colonials, and a dour, tweedy, very proper dyke opining that she would gladly sacrifice a million chimpanzees to spare one child one hour of pain.

Friday, there was always a party somewhere—but save it up for Saturday night in London town divine! First stop, the Green Door, where the female impersonators came on at 8 P.M. The onlookers were a motley crew—Irish grandmothers yowling with delight when the lovely ladies stuffed a wayward falsie back in place or hitched up a girdle. A few gay guys, sporting tank tops and tight Hong Kong jeans. Then Tretona's crew, mostly staff from the college, plus Helene-Claire's French connections. It was a working-class pub where everyone is friendly, but nobody pries.

On to the Chepstow Arms. The British were such wooden dancers that Tretona always felt good about her own efforts to be sinuous. Besides, there was a side room where you could even talk. And then at 1 A.M. when the disco closed (the British licensing hours sure put a crimp on decadence!) it was off to the coffee stand on Chelsea Bridge to watch the Thames in the moonlight and chat with the Pakistani chap at the chips stand who had a law degree but couldn't find a place as a barrister.

One could never tire of London, but Booneville! Well, everybody said Booneville was a good place to get work done. *If* you didn't overdose on boredom and just Rip Van Winkle your life away. Five summers now Tretona had gorged her soul in London. And five winters she had grumped and worked away in Booneville. Until one autumn a small poster appeared, flimsy paper but very clear:

OUR PLACE COFFEESHOP
114½ S. ROGERS
SPONSORED BY THE BOONEVILLE GAY ALLIANCE
TUESDAY WOMEN ONLY

An oasis for the parched, lonely gay traveler. Tretona had already checked out the Women's Studies Program—all fast-talking, middle-aged faculty. Great ladies, but whoever said most feminists were dykes hadn't been to Booneville! Then there was the Depot Saloon, literally on the other side of the tracks, and full of grizzled derelicts and a few tough-looking pool playerettes, who had been friendly enough when Tretona got up courage and ventured in one evening while it was still daylight, but not very—well, not very appetizing.

So, come Tuesday night it was with great expectations and debutante's quivers that Tretona peeked into Our Place. The small building had originally housed a used-clothing shop. Now there was a cheery poster on the side door, and inside, bare walls, Japanese lanterns, and a couple dozen women sitting on the floor. A guitarist was setting up. Tretona picked the most interesting clump and sat down on the edge.

There is a certain ozone flavor to dyke-dyke introductions. Will we be friends? Lovers? Rivals? Faces and eyes that are accustomed to wearing straight masks suddenly feel naked, vulnerable, brazen even when we meet our own kind in our own space. No longer protected from evaluation by our differentness, here we must at last subject ourselves to peer review.

Tretona's neighbor was from Connecticut and seemed pretty self-assured. She volunteered her name and chattered away about how strange it was to be west of the Hudson. But the University of Southern Indiana happened to be tops in Health and Recreation so here she was. Tretona liked her energy —and her tan—so when it transpired that Lynda played the banjo, Tretona started talking about how much fun it would be to get a string band together. She knew some lesbian songs from London and maybe . . .

"Sounds great. We could do it at my house." Tretona and Lynda turned toward the unexpected third party. "I've got a Martin and a twelve-string that somebody could use, plus it's all set up for taping sound on sound." And thus it was that Teresa Kowalski entered Tretona's life. Teresa not only had a Martin and a Sony but also a Mercedes, a Leica, and Tony Lama boots. Teresa wrote concrete poetry, did ceramic sculptures and photo montages, and peddled dope. She was also unemployed, extremely well read, and very funny. Tretona was a goner from the very beginning.

Not that she didn't work hard at trying not to fall in love too quickly. The string band rehearsed for two whole weeks before she and Teresa ran into each other at the yogurt ice cream place and had a lemonade that lasted three hours and a half.

Neither one could stop talking, Tretona about the wonders of London and how hard it was working nonstop for tenure when there wasn't anyone around Booneville who—well, who cared. Teresa had moans too—she was new in town and her lover had died less than a year ago in northern Wisconsin. Teresa made it all sound very mysterious—vague hints of defective brakes and FBI pursuit. Tretona got hints of dope rings and radical politics that had started back in anti-Vietnam days. She also couldn't figure out whether Teresa had been fired from her post office job up at Madison or had left it because she was broken up about her lover. In any case it was clear that Teresa could use some good home cooking but when Tretona tendered an invitation, Teresa just said she never tied herself down in advance—"catch you later." So Tretona bided her time. And when Our Place sponsored a body awareness workshop she even made sure not to get Teresa as a partner. God, tracing anybody's aura was a danger to her whole wiring system. To touch Teresa, to knead those arms, smooth her forehead, massage the temples and eyebrows and sinuses . . .

*   *   *

Big cities jade the appetite with their smorgasbord of poets, plays, kooky dance groups, strange political organizations, what-have-you. If one dish doesn't suit, never mind, try another. But in a small town, Christmas comes just once a year and if you don't choose wisely you're just shit-out-of-luck. And if the local gay coffee house gets taken over by weirdos, there is no other place to go.

So when the student activities board asked Kate Millet to come to Booneville and even let Women's Studies co-sponsor it and then someone from Our Place got herself on the reception committee, you know there's going to be some pushing and shoving. For a while it looked like a dyke takeover—Tretona as a woman faculty member was going to dinner with the speaker, maybe Teresa could be the official photographer, and Lynda was going to get another dyke to work sound and lights, chauffeur Kate to and from the auditorium, etc.

Of course, in the end the agent phoned and said Kate had a bad cold and must severely restrict her activities, and the technicians' union sent five people (at after-hours rates) to do *son et lumière*, and the Student Activities President—a fraternity boy—developed a sudden interest in feminist writing. But before the outside world intervened, there had been three meetings at Our Place in which Lynda was trashed for not trying to engineer a dyke-only reception for Kate. When Lynda said that just wasn't practical, someone shouted that it wasn't fair for white middle-class university types to have the only access to Kate. Then Teresa said hell, she was unemployed, it just depended on who had skills or something so that Lynda could make a case for including them, and someone mumbled, "Skills or a Mercedes?"

Tretona was actually relieved when a common enemy intervened. Thus it was with a diffuse belligerence (partly at the boy, partly at each other, and partly at Kate for even existing and thereby causing all the fuss) that a dozen odd dykettes lined the front seats of Alumni Hall. Tretona plopped down by Teresa.

"Where's your camera? Aren't you going to take any pictures? Not even for yourself?"

"Hell no." Teresa was glaring. "I might inadvertently stand in front of some proletarian dyke with her Brownie. Besides, the Leica is sensitive to bad vibes."

Tretona tried to be soothing. "Yeah, we did have a town/ gown split developing. That's really too bad."

"Well, it's inevitable. You can't expect good relations between RCA dykes and Radcliffe dykes—we're just too different." Teresa waved her hand vaguely up and down the front row.

Tretona obligingly scanned the crowd. "You can't tell by looking," she said. "Jennie Sue over there works in packing, out at Otis Elevator—never finished high school and she's got a nice sweater on. And look at the new tutor from the law school— torn blue jeans and a railroad cap and a plaid shirt. Or do you think there's an inverse relationship between—actually, I don't know what you're talking about."

Teresa was still impatient, but at least she had sense enough to lower her voice. "All dykes dress down, stupid. It's the chic thing to do and a way to identify yourself. No, I'm talking about downward mobility of the mind, of one's aesthetic nature." Tretona would have argued but some straight woman from the political science department had suddenly launched into an introduction. *". . . Sexual Politics . . .* the personal is political . . . and now the *Basement."*

"She sure managed to slip over *Sita,"* growled Teresa.

Tretona poked her into silence and then left her arm as close to Teresa's as she dared. But it was hard to be cuddly with Kate's voice at first carefully and clinically describing Sylvia's tortured death, and then calling out and pleading as if to the Spirit World, and then back to crisp political analysis: Sylvia's fate an extreme but inevitable result of patriarchy.

The speaker stood by the podium, all in black, her hair long and graying; her body seemed a receptacle for all the pain and injustice suffered by a thousand Sylvias. Ms. Poly Sci broke the spell by asking for questions and then people finally clapped—but what was there to cheer for, except to somehow send support to Kate—and then the fraternity boy did a filibuster question about conflicts between art and politics. Everybody booed, Kate said "Yeah," and then it was over.

It seemed understood that Tretona would catch a ride to the reception in the Mercedes. She decided not to comment on the car, nor on Teresa's flashy driving style.

"Kate was really feeling it, wasn't she? How can she travel all over the country doing that every night?"

"Well, she's a professional—she gets paid for it." Teresa's voice was matter-of-fact.

"Oh come off it. You know damn well that wasn't playacting. She said she was obsessed with Sylvia's story."

"What a wonderful obsession! So she has stigmata that

bleed on command. Big deal. I think people should work at being happy. I think we have a duty to rise from the slime. I don't care whether it's other people's slime or our own."

Tretona tried to compromise. "I think it would have been interesting to follow up more on Gertrude—do something like Truman Capote's *In Cold Blood.* Maybe we should go over to Indy sometime and look her up. Do you reckon she'd talk to us? I've never been inside a prison." Teresa just shrugged and parked up on the grass by the dormitory.

Students of hydrodynamics can probably write equations for the whirlpools that form around celebrated guest speakers. A few leeches grab choice inner-circle positions, smiling blankly as they adroitly adjust their footing. Keen fans dart in with genuine questions and then exit reluctantly, yearning for more sunlight but wanting to preserve the moment's intensity. Then there's the all-purpose autograph collector who juggernauts to the fore:

"Loved your book. [Or is it your books?] Though I've never bought it. [Them?] Never bought any, as a matter of fact. So would you autograph my steno pad?"

Tretona and Teresa bobbed around the maelstrom's periphery for a while, raided the punch table, and then joined a dyke outpost by the bay window.

"Maybe we ought to go rescue Kate," Tertona mumbled.

"How?" asked Teresa. "I suppose we could all stomp over arm in arm, mowing down sorority girls, *Ms.* magazine majors, and those other groupies."

Teresa had been leafing through a record cabinet. "Look, everybody. Guess what the dormies have. Sister Sledge." Howls of delight for an Our Place favorite.

"Get everybody. We're going to boogie." Teresa was in no mood to be argued with. Instant roundup of all dykes, be they RCA, Radcliffe or your Great Aunt Sally.

"WE ARE FAMILY!" Teresa spun the volume knob and grabbed Tretona.

"MAKE THREE," answered a dozen bobbing dykettes.

"You're absolutely mad, Teresa," gasped Tretona. "Whatever possessed you to . . ."

"The hedonic imperative!" shouted Teresa. And they hugged—forever—and then exploded into the writhing throng with claps and howls and stomps and great spasms of delight.

3.

Harlequin Daze

Zelda's rude squawks roused Tretona from memories of those mad breathless days when she first met Teresa—and found a gay niche in Booneville. What had she been? Innocent? Idealistic? No, not naive—more apple-cheeked and drunk from having a lover who was not going to disintegrate out of guilt or the sudden discovery of latent heterosexuality.

And then to have friends who smiled approvingly on clasped hands and cow eyes and to say when-are-you-two-coming-over? A cozy crucible of community support for the very intense reaction that was occurring between the two of them.

The straight world takes all this for granted: "Everybody loves a lover." Amendment: as long as they don't upset "the natural order of things." Can't have different races or the same sex, of course. But never mind the breeders and their funny ideas. Tretona was in love and for the first time there were no obstacles on the horizon—none that she saw, at least.

How wise we all are in retrospect. We tend to Monday-morning-quarterback past romances into episodes of completely embarrassing stupidity. Come on now, Tretona said to herself, while offering her finger to Zelda. (Zelda hissed and waddled back to the food dish.) Play it from the top. How did the fateful tapestry get woven in the first place? Were people dropping stitches all along?

*   *   *

"Arrgh." Four pegs thumping her stomach. Tretona brushed fur from her mouth. "Ho Chi Minh! Get out of here. Why can't you cats ever leave us dog lovers alone?"

Teresa turned over and stretched, waves swept through the waterbed.

"Come here, my little scrutible." Ho Chi Minh inspected his claws and ignored her.

"OK for you, Slopehead. I'll napalm your kitty litter." Violence is contagious. Tretona threw on a watery half-nelson. Teresa flipped away and started chewing on Tretona's toes.

"Hey, stop that!"

"Why should I? This little piggy tastes delicious. How about a blow job, little piggie?" Rude slurping noises.

"Teresa, stop that. I'll get seasick."

That was no idle threat. Once Teresa was rocking her to sleep, tongue all pointy, tracing her lips, inner, outer, up and down and all around. Then broad and flat, a scratching post for little pushy clitoris. Bodies undulating and pumping, Tretona feeling wave after wave, ascending and climbing until—she had to vomit, she really did. Oh my God, how do you explain this to a brand-new lover?

Teresa took it all in stride. At parties she would even make private little jokes—"Better take a Dramamine, Tretona—it's almost time to go home."

Teresa was pretty wonderful all around—except she wouldn't plan anything ahead. "What's on for today? When do you want to have dinner? Will you shop or shall I?" Any such request was laughed off, shrugged off, or flatly refused. Teresa seemed to live by some weird mixture of Ayn Rand and the Playboy philosophy. At first Tretona was was too much in love to care; then she tried rational argument:

"How can I make good decisions if you won't plan! It's silly for both of us to buy milk, or neither."

But Teresa was adamant about the value of spontaneity and not delaying gratification, and thought getting bummed out was a thousand times worse than a little inefficiency. Tretona almost said that wasting other people's time was a form of stealing and besides she got bummed out at Teresa's lack of responsibility . . . but she didn't.

Who can fight with someone who serves you baked Alaska in bed for breakfast . . .

who gets everyone in the middle of a thirteen-mile-long Dyke hike to take off their shirts and enter a body-painting contest . . .

who does a Gallup poll at an Our Place business meeting to find out the relative percentages of pink vs. brown nipples and then puts the results in the minutes . . .

who writes a letter to the *Advocate* about sex with pigs and signs the name of the president of Southern Indiana University to it . . .

who designs a wig for Halloween that looks exactly like a giant twat!

Most of the time Tretona was too out of breath to argue. She did place one limit, though—Teresa must not, under pain of death, distract her at the office. Tretona claimed it was mainly a question of getting work done. Teresa thought it was probably a closet problem. And maybe it was. Partly.

University people can be simultaneously very liberal about political questions and yet very conservative about general social norms. As far as Tretona could tell, most of her colleagues thought queers had the right to employment and housing and maybe even could raise their own kids *as long as they didn't flaunt it.* A guy from Western European Studies really got fired up one day at lunch. "If a school teacher maintains even a modicum of discretion, why would anyone even find out he was homosexual? Hell, heterosexual teachers don't go around advertising their sexual preferences! It should be an entirely private affair."

As a philosopher it was very easy and safe for Tretona to play devil's advocate. "What about your wedding ring, Heinz? Aren't you advertising a heterosexual relationship with Marlene? Better watch out, if it isn't sexual, you might be due for an annulment."

As usual when the subject turned to queers, everyone became very animated and vied for attention.

"But surely there is no need to be blatant," said Professor Kenneth Kilmister, a world-renowned expert on medieval agriculture. He started a long involved story about staying in a New York YMCA. It must have been before WWII and every time he went to the john, the same guy was in there brushing his teeth. No, that wasn't exactly true, once he was brushing his hair.

"Well? What happened?" Tretona tried to push the story forward. Must academics footnote even anecdotes?

"The second time I entered the lavatory (I had forgotten my towel) the man turned . . ." Kilmister's voice was shaking. The table tensed and Kilmister took courage: "The man at the sink turned slowly around—and he had the audacity to look at me —in that way they have." A shudder rippled through his body. "It was the worst thing that ever happened to me in my life."

Tretona played sympathetic. "It's strange, isn't it, how sometimes a glance can feel like an assault, like they're raping you with their eyes." Then, very gently, she inserted a tiny blade and gave it a wee turn: "That's how women feel, you know, all the time, when we go into a garage, or walk past those loafers down at the courthouse."

Again the table was tense but Kilmister accepted the point. "My goodness," he said, "I never quite thought of it that way before."

Heinz tried to lighten the mood. "With all this unisex business these days it's hard to tell who's what any more. Did you know there's a new guy in Italian who carries a purse? But I guess it doesn't mean anything."

"Except that his pants are too tight to have pockets!" someone giggled.

Tretona liked faculty lunches but she wondered what they all must think of *her*. From the very beginning she had tried hard to be both friendly and very eccentric. She reckoned that by the time people got accustomed to the birds in her office (zebra finches in honor of Darwin and the Galapagos), the Moroccan robes she wore to class, and the absence of chairs from her living room, they wouldn't have the energy to query anything else.

Sometimes Tretona had mad fantasies of going to lunch and reciting her weekend's adventures. "Teresa and I found the most amazing nook out at the quarries," she could have said. Big rock ... unbelievably warm for November ... stripped down ... just lying there smiling at each other, little fingers touching ... then voices approaching. Shall we scramble for clothes or hope they won't notice? ... Hey, it's a bunch of sorority girls. Teresa leaps up, buttocks gleaming, and waves a handful of colored leaves. "Sisters, join us—in autumnal rites. Diana is full and we are blessed." Blank stares as Teresa does little naked Nureyev leaps and chants a matriarchal mantra: "Diana, Lorena, Gertrude, and Alice."

Gasps and then a hasty exit. Tretona and Teresa serenade the retreating color-coded jogging suits with dykely howls and then nearly slide into the quarry from laughing.

"They ought to have had you in *Breaking Away*."

"I'm the madwoman of the Booneville quarry." Teresa squats monkey fashion and bounces up and down, rolling her eyes. "Here—you need an injection," says Tretona and inserts a cockleburr into the dancing twat. Screams, a quick tackle, Teresa's back scruntches too hard against the rock, and then fast mad sex, double penetration, hurry hurry, because we want it so bad, finish, finish, before the Delta Gammas come back, pluck pluck the autumn fruit.

How sweet it is afterward, buttoning denim shirts, lacing Timberland boots, retrieving the bouquet of perfect leaves. And how very difficult to preserve.

The Our Place crowd was getting more political. One Tuesday night they sat around tying to define "lesbian" and Lynda claimed it didn't really have anything to do with sex. Tretona remonstrated: "Hell, if you go with 'woman-identified-woman' as a definition you end up saying that nuns are all lesbians."

"Aren't they?" teased Teresa Kowalski. "I spent my entire

grade-school career praying that they were."

"That's my point," said Tretona. "You were praying that they were *lesbians*—romantic sexual lovers—not just 'women-identified,' whatever that means."

Lynda came back quickly. " 'Woman-identified' means putting women's welfare as your top priority, not just selfishly devoting all your energy to finding someone to sleep with."

"That's right," chimed in Christie, "romantic love is an atavistic remnant of our capitalist patriarchal heritage."

"Romantic love is a lot older than capitalism," Tretona protested. "It's in the Bible, Plato defines it, then there are all those troubadours in feudal times."

Christie sniffed. "Look at the language we use—we 'possess' lovers, they 'steal' our hearts away, cuckoldry is viewed as a particularly bad form of *theft*. As for the Bible, the same commandment that prohibits taking your neighbor's wife also proscribes the taking of his manservant, maid servant, or ox. In a patriarchal society all women are chattels. Lovers are just particularly prized possessions." She leaned back with an air of "the prosecution rests."

Tretona couldn't think of any comeback. Then Jennie Sue made a proposal: "I think we should love all women. And I don't think we should love one woman more than we can love all women—in our community I mean."

"Well, what are we waiting for?!" Teresa's eyes were snapping with mischief. "Line up, you lucky ladies. I'm going to love all of you. Right now." She grabbed Christie in a mock tango embrace, whirled to swoop up Jennie Sue, and the evening ended with everyone in great humor.

But that night Tretona couldn't go to sleep for thinking about it. *Was* there something selfish about loving Teresa so much, wanting to be with her so much, missing her over Thanksgiving vacation so much that she had to phone? And they had even been talking about moving in together. There had been only two problems—how Ho Chi Minh would get along with the dogs and whether Teresa could break her lease. But now what if the evening's discussion had affected Teresa?

Tretona gambled that Teresa wasn't completely asleep. "Honey?"

"Hmm?"

Damn, she should know better than to bring up something important when Teresa had already shut down for the night. But anxiety drove her on.

"Honey, what do you think about—?" Hell, what was she going to say—Do you believe in love?

"About what?"

"About that discussion tonight—you know, about not being bonded to one person."

"Oh, that." Teresa sounded bored. "It's always the have-nots who are in favor of redistribution."

"What do you mean?"

"Well, look at Jennie Sue. She's always moping around looking pathetic, hoping that someone will be nice to her. Of course *she's* in favor of watering down relationships."

"But you can't say that about Christie—she's real attractive."

Teresa rolled over. "Who wants to sleep with a lawyer?"

"Ooh, you're nasty."

"It's the same old lowest-common-denominator garbage. People think if they destroy something really magnificent, something really intense, there'll be more to go around. It never works. Now, go to sleep."

Tretona did, but not before resolving to stop being so affectionate with Teresa when other dykes were around, especially ones who didn't have lovers. Maybe it *was* being inconsiderate —sort of like slurping on a big ice cream cone on a hot summer day and not passing it around.

And so it came to pass that at massage class they were not partners (as they had been for several weeks) and that was when everything started to come unstuck—or so it seemed in retrospect.

Maureen's massage class, a prosaic name for a very electric occasion. Enrollment was limited to twelve people. No one ever missed and the waiting list was a mile long.

Picture it: Maureen, butt-long hair, barefooted, striped overalls with no shirt underneath, the meager furniture in her one-room efficiency stacked against the wall. The only light came from a lantern, incense covering the smell of kerosene and kitty litter.

Maureen yogi-legged on the floor, twelve dykes completing a circle, thirteen women in all. Lantern flickering as Maureen led the meditation, the consecration of ointments, the breathing, the focusing of energy and spirit, the loosening of body and mind.

Then Maureen would become intensely practical—a call for a volunteer (how we all longed to be Maureen's demonstration model), pointers on rhythm, exactly where to make the tiny circles. Always keep the oil warm, never lose contact with your partner. (Deft, complex maneuvers as she opened the oil bottle with one hand while stroking, and pulling, and soothing with the other.) Your hands should draw, not push—draw the blood toward the heart, pull out negative energy—now shake it off from your fingertips, never collect it in your own body. Break up knots of tension—dig them out, loosen the edges, and then demand that your partner release them, while you pound them away—see how they shatter and dissolve.

Each session they covered a different portion of the body. Tonight it was legs—and tonight Teresa was the model. Tretona watched as Maureen unbuttoned the Levi's fly, asked Teresa to raise her hips, and then slowly pulled off her jeans. Teresa never wore underpants—her belly glowed ivory and fur in the lantern light. Maureen sat between the legs, expertly draping one knee over her shoulder and then massaging the other thigh toward the heart, always toward the heart. How far would she go? Tretona almost couldn't look. Now define the groin—lots of tension where the hip joins the pelvis—rub it out, deep into the joint. Teresa's eyes were closed.

Just as the atmosphere became unbearably heavy, Fur Face,

Maureen's familiar kitty friend, streaked across the circle and pounced on a shoelace. Everybody giggled, Tretona threw Teresa a sweater, which she obligingly donned like a loincloth, and the demo ended.

Not quite knowing why (a fear of massagus interruptus?), Tretona allowed herself to be paired up with someone else. She watched as Teresa sought out Marilyn, a scrawny violin major. Then she turned to see whose legs would be on her plate. Christie was smiling as she took off her corduroys. "We're finally getting down to basics, aren't we?" Tretona fished for a comeback: "Those are very legal briefs you're sporting."

And so the moon set slowly on Maureen's cat and thirteen warm, oily dykes.

4.

B-Movie Break-up

With much reluctance I now turn to the story of how Teresa and Tretona split the blanket. It's not a pretty one.

Typically, the first sign of philandering is the broken schedule. Suddenly, one's lover is afflicted by an epidemic of late meetings at the office, traffic jams, and extra dental appointments. When she does finally show up, she is tired, testy, and prone to bedtime headaches. If one comes home unexpectedly from work, there are mysterious phone callers who hang up or leave no message.

Since Teresa had no normal routine, her symptoms were just the reverse. Suddenly she was tremendously organized— every morning spent in the darkroom over at the Student Union building, and violin lessons from Marilyn two afternoons a week.

The cover-up (as always) could have been detected by a third grader. "Gee, when did you get interested in violin? And lessons twice a week?" Mumbles from Teresa about being a guinea pig for Marilyn's practice-teaching project.

"And how is it going at the photography studio? When are you going to bring home some prints?"

"You know what a perfectionist I am."

And then Teresa's mother is suddenly taken ill and must be visited frequently on weekends. "Don't bother to phone—I'll be at the hospital most of the time."

But Tretona was very busy—her contract at the university

would be up for renewal next fall and all she really noticed was that the plan to move in together sort of got dropped. But their trip to Florida over Spring Break came off as planned—Tretona insisted on *that*. They took her car so the dogs could go, got a new trunk rack for the camping gear, and trekked all the way to Pensacola.

It was idyllic—white sand and gentle Gulf surf, even the jellyfish were golden. They camped out among scruffy southern pines, and the dogs chased coons and managed not to tree any skunks. There were shellfish dinners in town and woodsy breakfasts of oatmeal and raisins cooked overnight in a deep bed of coals. Even in March the Florida sun was too much for Yankee winter-bleached skins. Tretona spent one night swathed in Noxema and shivering. Teresa was unusually tender in her concern.

Tretona decided Teresa was really changing—for the better. She seemed much more thoughtful these days: phoned her mom twice from the camp grocery store and spent a lot of time on the beach writing letters to all her friends. One campfire night she turned especially serious and started philosophizing on what it meant to grow up queer.

"Gays are tougher than most people, don't you think, Tretona? We learn to take care of ourselves and don't let other people hurt us too much, don't we? We have to. In order to survive."

Tretona instinctively took the other side. "Well, I don't know. If a little kid never learns to trust anybody then it's pretty hard for her to grow up healthy and self-reliant."

"But I think it's important to learn *not* to trust anybody, not even yourself. That way you'll never be disappointed."

"Heav-vy. You don't really mean that, do you? You know what I think, Teresa? I think you've got to divide your life into two parts—life in the straight world where everything is weird and fucked and we play masquerades all the time, and life in the gay community where we can be straight with each other."

"Bullshit, Tretona. Get real."

"Now listen, I didn't say it was perfect, but . . . Look, here's an example. For a long time I was always falling in love with straight women—well, I don't know what you'd call them—straight, bi, or what. But the first thing I'd know, they'd be slipping away into some heterosexual thing and I'd get fucked over and there wouldn't be a damned thing I could do. I couldn't even blame them, not really. Hell, if they're straight there is no way I could ask them to be faithful to me, to honor all those whispered sexy vows to love me forever."

Teresa looked stern. "Oh, shit, Tretona. You should never take what a lover says literally. Those are just sweet nothings. They sound sweet and mean nothing. Nothing at all."

Tretona rushed on. "You're absolutely right about straight women. I don't know what they're doing—exploring, adventuring, testing themselves, maybe sometimes it's just raw exploitation, but all I know is that everything is different when you fall in love with a lesbian. Then it's real. Then you're both on the same wavelength, both trying to build something. Don't you think?" Tretona paused, not wanting to lose contact.

Teresa was impatient. "Damn it, don't be so goddamn naive. Dykes are people too. They can be fickle and erratic and not know what they want and . . ."

"Play it again, Sam," said Tretona, fiddling an imaginary violin. "Let's hear the badmouth dyke blues—we're oversexed but frigid, greasy, downwardly mobile shoplifters, psychopathic child molesters, corrupters of suffragettes, plus we let campfires go out. Quick, hand me some pineneedles. We'll never eat at this rate."

Teresa stared at Tretona, cleared her throat—and then went to fetch kindling from under the tarp. The rest of the evening was spent swapping ghost stories, wondering how Ho Chi Minh was getting along with Marilyn, and looking at the moon with binoculars.

"Hey, Tretona. I can see the American flag up there. One giant rape for mankind. Next they'll be putting up billboards.

Poor old Diana. Bet she never thought she'd have all those two-legged moon monsters tramping around."

"Yeah, it makes you feel funny, doesn't it? But I can't help thinking how pleased Galileo would be."

"Galileo? What's he got to do . . . ?"

"Well, he was the first to observe the mountains on the moon and all the clergy got in a snit because he said that heavenly bodies were no different from Earth. That was one of the things the Inquisition hauled him in for."

"Tretona, you really are weird. You really make me believe in that two-culture stuff." Teresa banged on her shoe with a stick of kindling as she continued. "Look what just happened. We look at the moon, I bring up Diana and you bring up Galileo. That's really typical."

Tretona was puzzled. "No, you brought up space travel— that's why I brought up Galileo."

Teresa kept staring at her boot. "We just really aren't very much alike."

"Hey, don't pick a fight." Tretona scooted along the picnic bench until they were side by side. "That's why I love you so much. Because you are so different—so wonderfully different." And she put an arm around Teresa and Teresa said she was all mixed up and then they were cold and dived into sleeping bags and watched the fire die down . . . and turn into ashen memories.

* * *

The willows turn pale yellow, then green. Tough little narcissi and cheeky hyacinths strut along Booneville sidewalks. Chickadees gossip about their winter in Carolina. In spring every young dyke's fancy inexorably turns to thoughts of—SOFTBALL!

Saturday afternoon: a panicky search for gloves and bats. Here they are stored under old magazines and unmended shorts. Hope the field won't be too muddy. Hope those bratty kids aren't out there flying their damn kites. Hope they'll let me play first base, maybe even shortstop.

And so with shining eyes and rusty elbows, a dozen dykes

congregated in Dunn Meadow. Tretona brought Teresa's mitt
for her but she didn't show, not for warmups, not for batting
practice, not even for the scrimmage. Rusty Mitchell, pitcher
and coach for the Xantippes, missed her too. "Hey, tell Teresa
she better show next time if she wants to play this year. Tell her
we need her bad. B-league is getting tougher all the time."

"I'll tell her. She had a violin lesson at eleven o'clock, but
I don't know where she is now."

Actually, Tretona had a damned good idea, and it was with
a mixture of concern and exasperation that she drove over to
Marilyn's apartment.

The roommate answered the door. "Marilyn? Sure, I'll get
her." Over to the closed bedroom door. "Hey, Mare. You got
company."

After a couple of minutes Marilyn slipped out, carefully
closing the door behind her—but not before Tretona caught a
glimpse of Teresa's bare bottom as she struggled back into her
Levi's.

"Oh," said Marilyn and clutched at the neck of her kimono.

Tretona switched into that wonderfully cool, efficient mode
that enables us to rescue drowning children and organize fire
bucket brigades without even thinking. In one motion she threw
open the door, picked up Teresa's boots and grabbed Teresa by
the elbow.

"The violin . . ." said Marilyn weakly.

"Hey, you can't . . ." said the roommate.

"Tretona, don't be . . ." said Teresa.

But like a mountain avalanche, mad with gravity, Tretona
swept Teresa out the door and into the car. Teresa babbled.
"You don't understand—I can explain—calm down for God's
sake—Tretona, stop—I want to get out."

King Kong, dumb animal, still knows he is wounded and
returns to his lair. So Tretona beckons Teresa—"Come." Up to
their bedroom—no, her bedroom—and at last the automatic
pilot switches off and now the adrenalin spews and fumes and
sprays.

"You fucking bitch," and she tackles her lover, bawling and embracing and wrestling her down. "Oh God, I can even smell her perfume on you." Pure rage, smash that beloved face—classic, open-handed slaps—movie perfect—now the right, now the left—some residual instinct not to maim, not to destroy.

Teresa's guilt turning to angry fear—a scream, a struggle, and then a sickening thunk as a head hits the casement.

"My jaw," says Teresa. Her lip is bleeding. "I'll take you to the hospital," says Tretona.

Once more on automatic pilot, racing through stop signs. "Are you going to be OK?" "It's swelling." How ordinary their voices.

"How did this happen?" said the nurse in green. Tretona wondering if she would be arrested. Could a convicted felon get tenure? Yet not caring really.

"Oh, I slipped and fell," said Teresa.

Damn you. Must I also be grateful? She had taken a breath to intervene when Teresa grabbed her arm. "Don't be a dolt—help me with this wheelchair."

And so the bloody ranks of queers close when the breeders converge. They even exchanged silent groans when the doctor introduced the inevitable boyfriend. "He is going to have a lot of explaining to do. You're going to have a beaut of a black eye."

The nurse was sharper. "Are you sure you want me to record this as an accident?" she asked Teresa. And then to Tretona, "You agree with that interpretation? These records are private, but if you folks wanted to press charges later . . ."

How handy it is sometimes that the whole world presumes that we too are heterosexuals. And that ladies are never violent.

I wish I could report a clean break, a tit-for-tat we're even (you broke my heart, I almost broke your jaw), a catharsis that really purifies instead of just intensifying the conflict with a lot of quotable quotes. But instead:

Marilyn called up Tretona and insisted she pay the emergency-room bill. Tretona said fuck you bitch—can't Teresa speak for herself. Tretona, meanwhile, phoned Teresa's landlord and pretended to be a neighbor complaining about Ho Chi Minh. (No pets were allowed.) Soon afterward Teresa and the cat both moved in with Marilyn and roommate. So Tretona wrote the city about the zoning law and multiple-occupancy regulations.

Then Tretona offered to pay the emergency-room bill after all and Teresa haughtily refused, then called up at midnight drunk and said why can't we all be friends. And Tretona sent flowers saying I just want you to be happy—and hoped like hell that Marilyn was allergic to roses and would sneeze all over her fucking gypsy violin.

You know how it goes. All of that love energy suddenly undirected, leaking over into anger, revenge, self-pity, self-recriminations—why was I so blind—I should have known. Why was I so thoughtless/inattentive—did I drive her away? Why didn't she tell me/warn me? Was I so unapproachable? Why was I so blind—circling over and over again.

And all of that sudden extra time, and extra play tickets, and unfinished joint projects. Who in hell would help her build the purple marten birdhouse? Whose oval sander would she use now?

No help at school. "Have you got an allergy?" Having worked so hard to convince her colleagues she was a self-sufficient old maid, it was hardly possible now to say talk to me, be nice to me, I'm all broke up.

And our lesbian sisters? Sadly, gently, but inevitably they all say the same: Honey, you didn't really expect it to last forever . . . Honey, we all have to do our own things—to merge and to grow and sometimes that leads us apart . . . Honey, monogamous marriage is a patriarchal concept—we have to create new forms, new possibilities. . . . Same old song, only the verses show any variety. Lynda's solo: "Find a new lover." Christie caroled, "Now you'll have more time for politics." Jennie Sue chirped brightly, "Why not do something creative like poetry." And then all together for the chorus: *Tretona, you've got to pull yourself together.*

But how? Her brain became a nocturnal animal, sluggish by day but gnawing and scuttering around in the middle of the night. It was impossible to eat right—even her beloved Kraft dinner had lost its soothing power. Dirty dishes, dirty clothes, erratic lectures, ambivalence about every social commitment, yet the thought of being alone filled her with intense anxiety. Pull herself together? You might as well try to take along an open beer on a roller-coaster ride.

Yet we do all bottom out eventually. In Tretona's case it can be dated precisely. At 3:15 P.M. (she noted the time because she was trying to decide whether to skip the departmental meeting), someone moseyed up to her table at the Daily Grind. "Mind if I join you?" Pain overload destroys all wit. Dumb gesture at the chair—a shrug.

"I'm Helen Murphy. You don't know me, but you were recommended to me for this project."

Tretona was interested enough to raise dull eyes.

"You know that Women's Awareness Week is coming up?"

No, I most emphatically did not and do not care.

"Well, I want to take some direct action to force people to be more aware of feminist issues . . . and I need someone to hold the ladder and stand guard and help out in general. Look, is it worthwhile for me to go on talking to you or am I totally off base?"

Talk to a Libra about *direct* action? Talk to a philosopher about action? Talk to an old-time, would-be monogamous dyke about feminism? Tretona couldn't imagine who had sicced Helen Murphy in her direction. It was all so ludicrous that she said YES and held the ladder while Helen defaced the Stop Abortion sign across the street from the police station . . . and spray-painted the windows of the jewelry store that had a display of dismembered female mannequins . . . and filled the keyholes of the Booneville porn shop with liquid steel.

It was like Halloween and WWII resistance all rolled into one. Afterward she and Helen went to the Waffle House for pancakes and giggled and scared each other about what would have happened if anyone had seen them. And became fast friends.

* * *

Give me a spot to stand on, said Archimedes, and I will move the world. Give me enough displacement in time, thought Tretona, and I can rationalize any bit of behavior. Now, two years down the pike, it was easy to see what had transpired in the Teresa affair. Scribbling furiously, with intermittent clucks in Zelda's direction, she noted the main points:

(1) Teresa was her first "real" lover. (Footnote: real means non-closeted and non-straight.) (2) Hence, although not a teen-ager, she made all the typical romantic adolescent faux pas. (3) List of mistakes: She disregarded the incommensurability of values like promptness and responsibility . . . she assumed without checking that Teresa was looking for permanence . . . she assumed after a few weeks that they were *de facto* married. (4) There were aggravating circumstances—no agreement in the lesbian community about the morality of relationships. And on and on.

Well, that just about ties it up, thought Tretona, chewing reflectively on her pen. Just gotta learn from the whole affair without getting cynical. I still think that Marilyn was a predatory bitch and Teresa was a lying coward. There are definite limits to what rational analysis can heal.

But what was going wrong now with Helen? Was she doomed to always being the historian, understanding everything but only after it was too damned late to do anything about the situation! What good is wisdom if it doesn't keep you from getting hurt? Come on Tretona, you met your first Amazon and then what happened?

5.

Matriarchy and Mungo Beans

World views are never adopted piecemeal. It's like sky diving. True, you can listen to lectures and look at movies or ride the parachute jump at the amusement park, but one day you just have to take the plunge.

And so Tretona fell from the bewildering anomie and gentle intellectual anarchy of the Our Place gang into the strange new world of Amazonia. A labyrinthine landscape of new vocabulary, new mores, even a new eschatology. What philosopher can resist an anthropological adventure through a new conceptual framework? Especially with a guide of legendary beauty, brains, and energy.

* * *

It was Tretona's living room but Helen was clearly in charge. Before anyone arrived she had removed the basketball poster (Why do you follow boys' sports?) and sighed over Tretona's record collection (Don't you support womyn musicians?). Now she was helping Tretona organize refreshments—trouble there, too. The cookies contained white sugar and the cups were made in Japan. (Boycott Whale Killers.) Tretona batted 1000 on the tea, though; luckily she had some weird herbal stuff with dried flowers in it that her brother and sister-in-law had brought back from southern France. She put it out in front and played down the Earl Grey.

Members of the Feminist Theory Ovular tromped in. Helen had described them as "harpies living on the boundary," but

they looked pretty much like ordinary dykes to Tretona. Lots of
hugs all around, chattering about car repairs, karate class, and
a new place someone had found that would give away manure.
Then Helen began.

"Womyn, you all know the university kicked us out of our
old room along with the Free University program. Martha is
checking our case out with a lawyer from Indy."

"Is she a feminist?" asked a tall dyke in a work shirt. Helen
looked at Martha for a reply. "Well, she seemed OK. She spe-
cializes in sex discrimination cases. Also, the first consultation
is free."

"I don't think we should get involved with a lot of *Ms.*
magazine liberals."

Helen intervened. "Look, Zak, we talked about all of this
last time and I thought all of the womyn here agreed. Martha's
just using the lawyer as a resource. Sometimes we have to inter-
face."

Mumbles of consensus.

"Anyway, in the meantime, I have met Tretona. We can use
her living room and there's plenty of room upstairs for child
care."

Shouts of All RIGHT! Tretona felt like blushing and tried
to think of something to say.

"How old are the kids?" she asked. "I've got a few toys for
toddlers, but nothing for tiny babies."

There was a sort of rustling silence. "Don't worry, we'll
take turns looking after them," said Zak. Helen was more can-
did. "There happen not to be any children yet, Tretona, but we
believe in spontaneously providing the facility. Womyn
shouldn't have to ask for their right to child care. We should
always offer. It was correct of you to bring up the toy question."
Tretona was half-worried that they might next set up a committee to collect toys for the nonexistent children, but Helen was
moving on.

"As you know, we have temporarily finished with retro-
spective investigations into the historical roots of matriarchy.

Now it is time to start building a new matriarchal society and for that we need Feminist Theory. I thought we might begin by reading some classics, old and new. How do you feel about that? Can we have suggestions?"

The first books mentioned were completely new to Tretona —gynecology and something about roaring within nature. But then Adrienne Rich's name came up and when someone proposed Simone de Beauvoir's *The Second Sex* Tretona decided to chip in.

"As long as we're doing philosophical classics, how about John Stuart Mill's essay on the subjection of women?"

She immediately sensed that something was wrong, but Helen was unflappable.

"We've decided to stick to womyn writers."

"Yeah, we've heard from the boys all our lives," someone shouted. Cheers.

Tretona knew she should shut up, but, goddamn it, this was her field.

"Well, it depends on whether you are interested in ideas or personalities. Mill's *ideas* on liberty, et cetera, were very influential on the British suffragette movement. And for what it is worth, he got a lot of his ideas from Harriet Taylor, just like de Beauvoir was influenced by Sartre, of course."

There was a confused hubbub about the personal being the political and men never being feminist, liberalism underwriting capitalism, the repressive nature of tolerance. . . .

Zak finally gained the floor. "I've said all the time that we need to add a class analysis to our gender analysis. You can't understand patriarchy without understanding class oppression. We ought to be reading Engels on the family and Lenin on . . ."

More hubbub: Marxists are the worst sexists of them all— patriarchy isn't just a bourgeois invention . . . but isn't that Engels's point. . . .

Helen waited for a tiny crack of silence to appear and then took charge.

"Womyn, we're building a new world view and a new

society. Not everything can be dealt with at once. We must use the best, the most reliable resources that we have. We all know and trust Mary Daly, right? How would you feel about starting there?"

The bonds of unity quickly reemerged. A hat was passed to pay for Xeroxes of recent reviews, book-sharing groups were constituted, and everyone started admiring Martha Morex's copper and brass miniature labrys, which, it turned out, had been her final project in a jewelry-making class.

"If I take the metal-working course, I'll make a life-sized Amazon axe," Martha said. "And carry it in the back of my van. Then if a boy bothers me . . . *whish!*"

A thrill went through the group, and Tretona shivered inside. Eventually, after more hugs and much joking, everyone straggled out. Only Helen made no move to go. Tretona hesitated. What she desperately wanted was emotional first aid—hold me, tell me I am wonderful and that nasty old Teresa can't hurt me anymore. But there was a surge of pride and hope that held her back. If I want to be friends with Helen—and I desperately do—there's no use in exhibiting my bruises right off. Mutual respect is a much better opening gambit than pity.

And so Tretona produced a bottle of Drambuie and two sherry glasses and carefully arranged some pillows on the floor. "That sure was an interesting group of people," she said politely.

"All womyn are fascinating," Helen said without a hint in her voice that she had just corrected Tretona. "At least they are if they don't bullshit themselves."

I wonder what that means, thought Tretona, but ignored it. "I was surprised there was no talk of our midnight vigilante raid."

"They don't know about it yet," said Helen. "I'm saving it as a surprise. The Daily Deadly is going to have a couple of really ignorant protest letters tomorrow—one from Doc Johnson's Marital Aids and the other from the Aid to Dependent Foetuses Society."

"Really? How do you know?"

"'Cause I wrote them. Then I called up the editorial office to complain some more and got a promise they'd print them."

"I'm not sure I see what you're doing, Helen. Is the plan for us all to write in to explain the issues?"

"Sure. But the main thing is to make sure we get some publicity. The paper isn't going to go around publicizing vandalism directly. However, if a *businessman complains*—that's news. Wait'll you see my letter on behalf of Doc Johnson. It's really wacko—full of all sorts of stuff about how pornography helps stabilize the nuclear family by preventing adultery and how it helped us win the war—kept up the morale, you know—hardened their resolve."

Tretona almost kicked over the Drambuie bottle with delight. "That's great—a perfect *reductio ad absurdum*. But doesn't the paper always phone back to validate letters?"

"I took care of that. I used your number."

"Hey, wait a minute!" Tretona's warning lights were flashing.

"It's OK," said Helen. "I knew you wouldn't be home. You never are during the day—that's when they'd call."

Little Miss Machiavelli, thought Tretona. This lady never misses a trick. But hell, I'm already an accomplice. "Say, I meant to ask you before. Why did you get me to go along instead of —oh, Zak or Martha, or any of those folks that were here?"

"To put it crudely, I wanted to see if you had any ovaries," came the immediate reply. "I saw you at the Kate Millet thing goofing off over by the record player. Then I heard you were a philosopher. We need your skills, so I recruited you."

Can't fault you on honesty, thought Tretona. But didn't you like me, too—maybe just a teenie little bit? Feeling flustered, she sought a rundown on the study group.

"So tell me about these Ovularians," she asked, proud that she was learning the jargon. "Who are they? How'd you all get together?"

"Well, most of us met at the Good Earth Co-op—you

know, working late nights bagging figs or measuring out carob. Then we started networking, and discovered that womyn workers always ended up cleaning out the peanut-butter bins and handling food, while the boys did all the ordering and bookkeeping. You know how they always pig the good jobs, though I'd rather work with vegetables than numbers, but that's not the point. Anyway Zak's boyfriend was the coordinator so we requested . . ."

Tretona was incredulous.

"Zak's *what?* Isn't she a dyke?"

Helen smiled patiently. With the air of a mathematics teacher demonstrating that there really are just as many even numbers as integers, she explained:

"Zak's a political dyke—she didn't fall in love with her gym teacher or get a crush on the girl next door or any of that stuff. When she was an adult she just analyzed everything and decided she wanted to be a dyke—that was later, though."

"Better late than never, I suppose." Tretona sounded nonchalant, but inside she was all ajumble. Could someone decide to be a dyke? She knew a lot of straight women who played around with lesbians, but they weren't anything like Zak—they would never label themselves that way. Somehow she just couldn't imagine Zak with a boyfriend—her strong face, big bones, rough hands. Of course, there she went again, drawing conclusions from stereotypes. Still, if there ever was anyone who looked like a dyke, moved like a dyke, talked like a dyke, surely it was Zak.

Then Tretona really got worried. What if Helen were a political dyke too? Before she had time to analyze why that would make a difference, Helen had answered her question, sort of.

"Hard to imagine Zak ever being in love with a boy, isn't it?" Helen said. "But one of the really exciting things about our group is to watch womyn undergo transformations, how they change and grow. Take Martha Morex, for example."

And there followed an incredible tale about Martha's having been in a convent and how she had been a quiet little vegetarian pacifist when she first joined the Good Earth. "All she would talk about was mung beans and folic acid. Now she's a real warrior, good at karate, and I don't think she's kidding about making an Amazon axe. Womyn have been denied weapons as well as tools."

A feminist jihad? thought Tretona. A holy war?

"I think changing her name was a big spiritual step for Martha. She used to be named Martha Moreman."

"Oh, I see what's coming," said Tretona, a little disgusted.

"It's a little more interesting than you think," Helen pushed on. "So when we read Elizabeth Gould Davis about how womyn were the first sex and men were just mutants, Martha got teased a little—people called her 'More-mute.' It wasn't very sisterly really. But Martha snapped right back and said her name was 'More-X'—X for X-chromosome, get it? And bless her feminist heart if she didn't go down to the courthouse and change it legally. It cost her fifteen bucks."

A dozen objections sprang into Tretona's mind: Names are conventional. Only primitive people think names have magical power. Words don't matter as long as we all use them the same way. Sticks and stones may break my bones, but words . . . But somehow she didn't quite dare to get into an argument with Helen. Not yet anyway. And words obviously did matter to Helen. She chose more neutral ground.

"So is the claim that men evolved after women? That's pretty speculative, isn't it? Just sounds like an inversion of the old Adam-before-Eve story to me."

Helen's eyes flashed but her answer rolled out smooth as silk: "Well, you obviously haven't read Davis' book. All evolutionary scenarios are speculative, of course, but Davis makes out a pretty good case. The Y-chromosome is just a broken-off bit of the X, you know. And of course almost all academic biology has been done by men—although even they admit womyn were the first to domesticate plants and animals."

"But having two sexes is a very common evolutionary

strategy. It's a good way of getting genetic diversity. Gee, you find sexual dimorphism in all sorts of lower animals and plants. Sex is a lot older than people. You can't just say the Y-chromosome is a little castrated mutation of the X. That doesn't make any biological sense at all."

"Well, it makes a lot of sense to womyn." And with considerable feeling Helen told about how liberating these ideas had been to the Ovular. "We had already seen how early matriarchal forms of social arrangements had been smashed by the violence of war and patriarchal religions and then to see the parallel in biological development—it was all very impressive."

"But it's phony biology. You're just spinning myths."

Now Helen was really serious. "Don't ever doubt the power of myths, Tretona—I mean womyn's myths, not the bullshit stories we grew up with. We have to build a feminist mythology and recover womyn's herstory. What difference does it really make how the two are intertwined? Both are sources for spiritual growth and political action."

Helen's voice was so vibrant and her brow so smooth that Tretona almost bought the argument. But as soon as she looked down at her liqueur glass her normal thought patterns took over. Hadn't the Nazis built their own mythology—Wagner and all the Norse war-gods and stuff? And how about the way the Stalinists had rewritten the history of science so that all the really important discoveries were made by Russians? Of course those distortions and fabrications were done for evil purposes and feminism wasn't evil, but still. . . .

Helen read her expression. "You find this pretty hard to understand, don't you?"

"Well, when you've been taught all your life to be critical and analytical, you can't just turn it off. . . ."

"No one is asking you to turn off the left side of your brain, Tretona. I just want you to turn on the right hemisphere too."

And then their right cheeks touched and the right sides of their mouths brushed and nibbled and clung and right hands on right breasts—oh Amazon show me your sinister secret side and the deep centers of your body.

The paradox of sexual attraction: it is the strongest, least resistible passion in the world, and the most fragile. An unexpected odor, a flicker of inattention, an intrusive thought and poof!—the transcending magic vanishes and one is left with sweaty distended tissues, needs, appetites, techniques, skills, and even the will to carry through, but no poetry. It happens to everyone—at least to all of us romantics: a sort of spiritual impotence which may or may not be accompanied by physical disinterest. Yet we always feel guilty about it, or short-changed.

And so Tretona tasted Helen's mouth and found it sweet and firm, not cigaretty and a little slurpy like Teresa's, and immediately missed Teresa like hell and was angry at herself for doing so and kissed with new resolve and Helen very gently pulled her mouth away and hugged her very tight and said how wonderful it was to have a new friend and she knew they would be great pals and partners—and went home, leaving Tretona to wonder how long Teresa's mark would mar the surface of her mind.

* * *

To lose a lover is to lose a way of life: even softball is too painful, for how can one peg a quick throw to first base when your ex is standing on second and your rival (your successful rival) is sitting demurely in the stands (protecting her little violinist hands)? Mutual friends have divided loyalties and show it. So it's much more convenient for all concerned if somebody has the good grace to split. So it was with some gratitude that Tretona became an adopted Amazon, Helen's special protégée.

There was a lot to do—giant potlucks (once Tretona counted sixteen different quiches!) and weekly volleyball games out on Gnaw Bone Ridge. Jenny and Molly owned seven acres near a state forest and every Sunday afternoon would find venerable Volkswagens and other dykemobiles bouncing along back roads into the Hoosier heartland. Only the coon dogs knew how foreign the invaders really were and they would yap and howl, trying in vain to rouse their redneck owners who were lazing inside of dented, faded housetrailers, watching TV in front of a fan.

The road narrowed and turned and tunneled through a stand of scruffy timber before—LO! a lavender mailbox, up a lane and there was the teepee! Jenny and Molly worked in town but lived on their land and chopped and cleared and bush-hogged and planned a cabin to be powered by a windmill generator.

Everyone shared their dream and came out resolved to pitch in and help, but generally ended up burning more firewood than they cut and tracked mud into the teepee and walked on the garden by mistake, but Jenny and Molly loved the company and the enthusiasm. Besides, all those people running around scared the snakes away.

Tretona had heard all about Sundays on Gnaw Bone at the Feminist Theory class, but it still took her breath away. She had ridden out with Helen, of course, who seemed oblivious to the natural tempo of a Memorial Day weekend. Helen had just discovered some early Zionist essays that advanced a theory of Jewish separatism, why it was necessary for Jews to isolate themselves and rigorously enforce community standards. Tretona tried to argue that American lesbians were in quite a different situation, but to no avail. Helen had the steering wheel firmly in hand and cleverly used the bumps and ruts both to emphasize her own points and to obliterate Tretona's.

It was with great relief that Tretona abandoned the dusty abstractions of Helen's pickup truck for the warm green pasture on top of Gnaw Bone Ridge. A dozen dykes looked up and hollered hello when they drove up. Bronze breasts, cut-offs, and hiking boots. For a moment they looked like Israeli soldiers. But then the only-in-America content came quickly into view: Zak and Molly were passing a football back and forth. (Isn't football awfully patriarchal? Tretona wondered.) And what foreign legionnaires use Styrofoam cups to drink beer from an iced keg?

Not knowing anyone very well and feeling lazy, Tretona sat down by a stump and prepared for some serious body appraisals. It's not often, I think, that dykes systematically evaluate flesh-and-blood *bodies*. We can do it at dog and horse shows, of course, looking for that subtle combination of conformation and spirited movement that adds up to top honors. But when it comes to people—is it a taboo that intervenes? A result of a lifetime of revulsion toward the beauty-contest aspect of our culture?

Anyway, it was with some effort that Tretona let her eyes linger frankly and analytically on the volleyball players whooping around on the makeshift court. I don't know these people, she thought. And I can't talk to them just now. So what's the harm on a sultry day at the end of May in appreciating physical beauty?

Breasts demanded immediate attention. Look at that slim strong athlete—her breasts were her only concession to softness, a gentle contrast to the firm arms and ribcage. She would hold you very tight but your cheek would find a sweet, sweet cushion on that chest. Ooh! look over at those round bouncy ones, fairly crying out for nibbles and wee pinches.

Helen slid down beside her. "Having fun?" Tretona jumped a little, recovered, almost said Which do you fancy? and settled for "They're really playing hard, aren't they?"

Helen seemed to have a little speech poised for delivery: "It's really wonderful to see womyn using their bodies freely, not worrying about the constraints patriarchy places on female athletes. Look at Molly spike that ball—she can leap and swing with all of her strength because she no longer believes that womyn lack coordination."

Tretona's bullshit detector was flashing like crazy. She cautiously disagreed. "Gee, I never worried about looking too strong or looking unfeminine. My problem was just the opposite. Since I was a dyke, I figured I should be super *good* at sports. I used to send off cereal box tops for all those Breakfast of

Champions booklets on baseball and swimming and everything. But, hell, I never did have any wind and I guess my reflexes aren't very fast—I never was very good at pinball. Anyway, I was always a little hung up about sports, but it wasn't the little ladylike feminine model that I couldn't live up to—it was my ideal of what a dyke should be."

Helen looked interested, so Tretona rushed on. "Now, I know some dykes who were good athletes and they were scared, too. But they were always afraid that someone would guess. I don't think any dyke I know ever worried about all that feminity crap." (Oops, she thought, have I just negated *your* experience, Helen?)

Helen was matter-of-fact. "You have a valid point. That's another awful aspect of patriarchy, especially under capitalism. Always setting up impossible standards and whipping you if you don't achieve them."

Jeez, Tretona thought, why do you mouth this weird mixture of platitudes and absurdities? And so she grabbed Helen by the hand and together they invaded the game. A world of dust and sweat, sun in the eyes, broken fingernails, ridiculous shouting matches over shirt-marked boundaries and whether the serve was in. A world of make-believe competition and transient alliances (as people switched sides), but the physical exertion was real and so was Helen's pain when someone made a crazy leap and came down full force on her instep.

Tretona crashed the circle of solicitous onlookers and took charge; Zak was dispatched to get a sailor cap full of ice, and Rhonda sent off to the teepee for medicinal brandy. Martha fetched a cushion and blanket from the pickup. But it was Tretona who lifted Helen to her feet and draped the invalid's arm around her own strong shoulders. Together they three-legged it over to the nearest tree.

How sensual it is to take care of someone, to prop up the swelling foot, to tender ice packs and caresses, to ask if it hurts, to soothe and cluck and say what a shame it happened, and on such a beautiful day. And the eager nurse really is sorry her beloved is in pain, but if it had to happen, how wonderful that I am here to take care of everything.

And so Tretona passed the afternoon, her long legs barricading the poor sore foot away from the traffic of well-wishers and sharing their offerings of fruit, cornbread, and macaroni salad.

And although it was the furthest thought from her responsible conscious mind, somewhere in Tretona's psyche the erotic calculus was operating: If I can nurse your wounds, I can take care of your needs. If I can drive your pickup home skillfully, finding the gears and missing the potholes, then I can make love to you. Surely all of this competency and efficiency will compensate for my political ineptness.

And so it came to pass that Helen stayed all night at Tretona's house (fewer steps), where Tretona laid soft pallets down by the hi-fi speakers and played Cleo Laine and Emmylou Harris and fed Helen popcorn (to neutralize the brandy) and talked nonstop about her research and how good the graduate students in her department were. Until Helen smiled wanly and complained of a little headache which somehow, Tretona knew, was a sign to kiss her so compellingly that all pain was forgotten —or eroticized.

* * *

Notes for *Chapter N+1* of a Joyful Sex Manual: The Sprained Ankle as Love Aid. It clearly designates one partner as bottom, thus eliminating ambiguity about leadership. It acts as a natural constraint, thus inviting geometrical innovation while inhibiting uncontrolled flailing about. As a spot of unquestionable vulnerability it symbolizes the complex mixture of trust and fear that accompanies all lovemaking. May I kiss that sore, swollen purple wound? Even touch it like so with my teeth? No, no, I'd never hurt you. Feel me through your wound—it will magnify the slightest brush a thousandfold.

And so Tretona swooped up and down the moaning Helen, pull and maul those lips, find the tongue, dominate it, strain it through teeth, probe its roots and along the sides—ooh, almost tickles—meanwhile breasts warming on back burner, plumped into tense pyramids by fingers and palms, rubbing, kneading till they rise up thirsty, straining for the tongue which wets—wispy cool goosebumps then slowly swallowed into that warm wanton mouth—nipple tumbled round from rough roof to teeth to mothering tongue, dizzy with delight—meanwhile fingers on reconnaissance mission, tips sliding through underbrush—any place to hide? Oh ho, what have we here, warm wet slide, play out here a minute—a soft sculpture, climb up, poise on sensitive button top, pulses, shudders, can't take it, down, down forever into place so deep and firm—a tunnel of love—quick come out —find the button-button-button, who has the button—I have it says the tongue, see I can push it to and fro, a neon bubble —gentle now—but to no avail the greedy lips pounce and fingers crying come down here it's better—watch my rhythm— in quick, and out ever so slowly and then dive to very bottom, hold as long as—out ever so slowly—oh dear button let me kiss you, suck you up, so sweet, petit morceau.

Helen's hands pulling up Tretona's head and embracing her neck with fearful intensity—can't take it, please stop—but again somehow knowing to kiss her so completely and peacefully but leave hand in place drumming, throbbing until their bodies rose in rainbow salute, and the pot of gold glowed and beamed and quivered with its own beauty.

* * *

Helen moved in the next day. It was her idea. Tretona demurred mildly: Gee, that's great, but do we really know each other well enough to . . . ? But Helen laid out the terms very clearly. We're already friends. We work well together. Much more efficient to live together. If there's any problem, I'll move out, of course. There should be no question of one of those silly adolescent break-up scenes. I don't believe in romantic overcommitment. I love you and respect you and will behave in accord with those deep feelings.

It was a good speech. Tretona half wondered if Helen had already given it on previous occasions. Mainly, though, she wondered what would happen if she fell prey to a "romantic overcommitment." Still, she'd gotten burned once. And who could be against a relationship founded on integrity, respect, and reason? And who would think twice about living with an Amazon named Helen?

6.

Anger Rising

That first summer with Helen was a time of enormous productivity. Tretona was in a pre-tenure flurry and religiously spent six hours a day writing in her air-conditioned office. By midafternoon she was exhausted and either staggered over to the university pool and ogled the co-ed lifeguards or drank iced Red Zinger at the Runcible Spoon and doodled around with ideas for a Gay Studies course that she'd gotten roped into team teaching.

Helen got off at five and then the day really began. There were intimate little vegetarian barbeques on the patio with Zak and Martha, the backyard dotted with tomatoes growing in barrels and five-gallon buckets full of cucumber vines. Every spare corner had been spaded and planted with kohlrabi and pepper plants. Onion sets bravely grew around the base of the lilac bush. The dogs resented not being able to pace the fences and couldn't understand why the soft diggable dirt in the strawberry bed was off limits.

After everyone was sated on Helen's Heavenly Spuds, grilled corn, and the cheap Rumanian wine that every dyke in town drank (these were the days before teetotaling became politically mandatory), conversation would always meander around to politics: whether men were innately violent, and what would happen if womyn flew off in a spaceship and founded a new society. Tretona would argue that an Amazon utopia had no more chance of surviving than any other visionary scheme because women were basically no more civilized than men. She generally got shouted down, which rudeness, she never failed to remark, proved her point.

More interesting (or at least less predictable) were the anecdotes of sexual harassment. Everyone had stories to tell: about grandmothers who were ignominiously pulled out of the house by the nose to inspect Pop's new horse, great-grandmothers who had their own land and grew wheat on it for white bread but whose husbands sold it at the mill and brought home cornmeal instead. Stories of intelligent mothers who stayed home from college, watching duller brothers take their place and quit after three semesters. Memories of academic advisors who counseled their sisters out of geology and into geography. Stories of school-teacher aunts who never became principals. A litany of relatively minor injustices—yet each the tip of yet another iceberg of lifelong exploitation and powerlessness.

One night Zak commented on this paradox of the insignificant become significant. "In a way I feel weird about complaining about little things. Like that story I just told about the automotive guy who wouldn't believe me about 'seventy-four Datsuns having a different ignition system. When you think about all the womyn who get raped or killed or beat up every day, or the secretaries who have to put out for their slimy bosses, compared to that, my little beef about some grease jockey's not taking me seriously is pretty small potatoes."

Helen quickly filled in the connections. "But they all stem from the same root problem: patriarchy."

"Yeah," said Martha, "it's just that some outbreaks are more virulent than others."

"Gee," said Tretona, "to me the differences between murder or rape and a surly salesman are so enormous that I don't see the point in lumping them all together. Lookit: your salesman wasn't violent, he wasn't even insulting. He didn't even do anything that you could complain to his boss about. You just felt he wasn't taking you seriously. You have no real evidence that he treated you the way he did because you were a woman

—maybe he doesn't take any amateur mechanic seriously."

"Don't kid yourself," said Zak. "There's no way he would have been so damned arrogant with a man."

"You're probably right, Zak. I really think you are right, but see, the point is he didn't *do* anything to show he was being sexist. He didn't call you a dumb broad or anything, so that means you couldn't confront him with it."

"The hell I couldn't," Zak replied. "If I'd been on my toes I'd have read his beads. I should have just said, Hey, boy, don't be patronizing with me. This womyn knows more about Datsun trucks than your brain could ever comprehend."

"I can't think of a worse strategy," said Tretona.

"Why? Are you afraid he's gonna punch Zak out?" Martha was fierce in her loyalties. "Zak's tops in self-defense techniques."

"Look," said Tretona, "it rarely pays to get hostile and start escalating things. Either he put you down on purpose or he didn't. If he was just having a bad day your little attack wouldn't accomplish anything, he'd just think you're crazy. And if he was trying to needle you, he'd be absolutely delighted to get such a big rise out of you."

"I'll give those bastards a rise. A good karate chop to the adam's apple would be very uplifting." Zak's violent gesture scared Bebop and the dog slunk over to the far side of Tretona's lawn chair.

"The boy's conscious intentions are completely irrelevant," said Helen. "Every male in our society has imbibed patriarchal assumptions—even with their mother's milk, I'm sorry to say. We need to expose it everywhere."

Tretona just shook her head and then poked a stick at the charcoal as if to change the subject.

"I don't understand why you're always so critical of your sisters." Martha's voice had a labrys edge.

Tretona tried to think of what to reply but then the words came tumbling out on their own. "If you want to change some-one, you have to know where they are coming from, and you

have to let them save face. So you say, 'Bet you have to put up
with a lot of mechanical morons in this job.' Then maybe he'll
smile. Then you say something like—'Have many women cus-
tomers? My friends and I are starting to get into auto mainte-
nance and we really like it. I bet there's a whole new market
developing. What do you think?' Then if he says something
weird, you let him have it."

"Uncle Tom," said Martha.

"More like Aunt Sally," chorused Helen. "Tretona, you're
falling into the old trap—that women have to adjust to little
grown-up boys' foibles and smooth everything over."

"Look, if you just want to rant and rave, do it your way."
Tretona scratched Bebop's ear for support. "I reckon it's the
same as housebreaking a dog—if they shit on the floor, you
clobber them. But first you have to catch them in the act."

Everyone laughed and Martha launched into her latest
Amazing Amazon Animal Fact—certain female insects had the
ability to light up in a pattern that attracted male fireflies. "Then
when the horny little guy comes cruising over with his swollen
glowing abdomen, she devours him." There were shrieks of
delight, but Tretona couldn't help picturing the matriarchal
mandibles dripping with pale green phosphorescence.

Inside the phone was ringing. Tretona, clowning a bit in
case there was any residual tension, crawled through the doggie
flap at the bottom of the screen door to get in.

"Hello," she gasped. The caller stammered a little. "Er
. . . is Tretona there?" Three little words, but the voice was
unmistakable. It was Tretona's turn to pause, realizing that she
could get out of talking, but deciding not to.

"It's me, Teresa. What can I do for you?" Her own voice
was amazingly calm, but her heart wouldn't stop pounding.

Although four months had passed, the reservoir of mangled
feelings was still plenty full. Impossible to sort out. Hope of
reconciliation? No way that could happen. Anger at having her
expectations torn into shreds and stomped on? Surely she had
worked that through. No, it was more primitive—like a dog that

has been bred for generations to wag its tail and then learns that its every sign of friendship and loyalty triggers an electric shock.

So, Tretona responded gingerly to Teresa's "Just wondered how you'd been" with a noncommittal "Doing OK. Working hard. How 'bout yourself?"

It was not like Teresa to be so indirect. Some ramble about the forthcoming BGA conference (it seemed some folks from Our Place had formed a Booneville Gay Alliance that had somehow gotten University recognition). "Tretona—I'm not doing very well. I know I have no right to ask, but—could we meet and talk? I'm in trouble, kind of—and I don't know what to do."

How strange it is that when we already feel emotionally ripped off, the very best reconciliation move is a request that we give even more. Yet forgiveness requires the right power balance. A slave victim cannot forgive his oppressive master unless he assumes a position of moral superiority.

Tretona's mind raced—should be cool—for a moment she relished the chance she'd been offered to say no, but instead, "I could meet you, I suppose."

"Oh, 'Tona, thanks, I'm at Mother Bear's."

Who said anything about meeting you tonight? I need time to prepare. Somehow, though, through her apprehension and curiosity and magnetized helplessness, Tretona did manage to get the meeting place changed, partly just to exert a little power but mainly so that every other dyke in town wouldn't be dropping by their booth doing double takes. "Make it the Trojan Horse, would you? I'll be there in fifteen minutes."

It was only after she hung up that she realized that Helen's gang had been boycotting the place because their T-shirts sort of looked like contraceptives. Oh never mind; they had damned good baklava.

Tretona combed her hair at the kitchen sink, thought about going upstairs and brushing her teeth, but poured a shot of whiskey and sloshed it around her mouth instead. Then, standing at the back door: "Guess what? That was Teresa." Helen made no acknowledgment. "She's got some big deal problem—

guess I'll go talk to her. Want me to pick up some ice cream while I'm out?" Helen sat silent. Zak and Martha took the bait and yukked it up, but Tretona made one last attempt to get Helen's eye.

"Pistachio nut OK?" That was Helen's favorite flavor.

Tretona deliberately took the long way downtown—she mustn't arrive first. Fidgeted in the car cleaning out the glove compartment until seventeen minutes had elapsed and she couldn't breathe and had to go in. Paused at door for stage entrance—then saw Teresa sitting at the bar, head tipped down, inspecting the pattern of rings made by her beer glass.

"Hi." Tretona wished like hell she could think of something to say, but Teresa seemed to have an agenda. After they found a table she bombarded Tretona with questions. How had the dahlias turned out? Were they all one color? Had she finished her paper for the PSA on time? Did Bebop still attack the postman? Was the house really going to require a new roof?

Tretona was puzzled and a little annoyed—she was almost going to ask Teresa if her mom still got conveniently ill when Teresa suddenly stopped: "What I really want to know is how *you* are? No one ever sees you anymore, since you started running around with those weird separatists."

"Hey. Watch it. They are OK really." And Tretona told about Zak, who drove a city bus and could fix anything on wheels. ("You ought to have her check out that sputter in your Benz.") And she described Martha Morex who worked on the building-and-ground crew at SIU. ("She may have separatist politics, but that doesn't keep her from taking on a nontraditional job with a bunch of rednecks.") Not quite knowing why she made no mention of Helen.

The longer the conversation went on, the tenser Tretona felt—too many echoes from the past. She couldn't decide which was more painful: gentle memories of the good times that were no more, or the searing flashes of those awful moments. Finally, Teresa got down to it. "Tretona, you're always so good at analyzing things." Teresa picked up a matchbook and started pushing spilled sugar into neat square-sided mounds.

"I don't know who else to talk to."

A sugar pyramid started to dissolve as it touched moisture from the beer glasses. Tretona shifted her back against the wall, sat sideways in the booth, and waited.

"Marilyn is stepping out on me."

It was canoeing in rapids—crazy currents—no patterns to the feelings: now you know what it feels like, Marilyn always was a bitch, don't come back to me, would you be more serious now, no too late, poetic justice . . .

And finally she looked at Teresa's face swollen with pain and shot out into the calm waters of sympathy and caring.

"Teresa. I'm sorry. I really am. Who's the other woman—or person—involved?"

"You don't know her. It's Cynthia Du Bois. She's an Opera major." Teresa was tight-lipped, but calm.

"So they met over at the music school?" Tretona stuck to the safe factual level.

"Yep. Rehearsals for *Marriage of Figaro*. Marilyn's in the orchestra and Cynthia plays Carabino, the pageboy who's in love with the countess. She's a contralto."

Tretona was really fishing for something to say. "I don't know anything about opera. Is that a big role?"

Teresa's face was working now, visibly masticating the bitter message. "Yeah. She's good. She's black." Incipient tears but no release.

"Let's get out of here." Tretona slapped down bills and pulled Teresa after her. Now, outside, pausing in the vestibule of Howard's Bookstore.

"OK. So Cynthia's black and she's a good singer . . . when did this all . . . ?

Teresa clutching at her elbow, bawling and blubbering, driving the toe of her boot into the wall over and over.

"I hate her. I hate her. You can't imagine. I hate her because she's black. I never thought I was prejudiced. In high school I did drugs all the time with . . . but when I think of her kinky

pubic hair and Marilyn . . . I just hate her so much. And I don't
know what to do. I'm so ashamed. I couldn't tell anyone else."

Tell me, philosopher, can you parse pain? How do you
dissect and weigh emotions? What proportion of her hatred
concerns ordinary old betrayal and what percentage is racial?
Imagine instead a redhaired pubic mound under Marilyn's fair
cheek. Can you measure the pain reduction? Or is this self-
flagellation really a diversionary tactic so you don't have to face
up to the central issue? Can you even analyze the direction of
the hatred vector? Does it really point toward Cynthia, or
maybe more toward Marilyn? Even the qualities are unclear. Do
you feel anger, pain, stupidity, hurt pride, loss, regret, all of the
above, and in what ratios?

And so Tretona cuddled and soothed and stroked and patted—the ancient animal language of comfort.

* * *

She forgot the ice cream—too late for it now anyway. Helen was
propped up in bed reading. Formal recognition over her half
glasses. "How was Teresa?"

"Not so good. Marilyn's seeing someone else."

Helen sighed. "The old monogamy mirage, uh? When will
people ever stop imagining things that aren't there?" She turned
back to her magazine.

You arrogant fuckhead, thought Tretona. Since when did
you become an expert on what's real.

* * *

Torpor. Mildew. Humidity Hoosier style. No dyke in Booneville
could afford an air-conditioner. Bromine haze enveloped the
outdoor pool. Tretona wondering if she should put ice cubes in
the aquarium—the book said to keep tropical fish between 75
and 80 degrees. The dogs were spread-eagled on the basement
floor. Only Zelda the cockatiel seemed oblivious to the heat,
perching for hours on the sunniest window ledge and shrieking
as usual when Tretona gave her a spray bath.

Tretona was looking forward to seeing the Feminist Theory
group. Talking to Teresa had made her realize how much she

really liked this motley army of Amazons. Tonight there was going to be a big synthesis of what they had read so far. Helen had been writing madly for two days. The back of her notebook had all sorts of key words on it—power, violence, boundary, myth, anger, bonding. Occasionally an item got crossed off. Tretona didn't know if that meant rejection or that the concept had already been incorporated into Helen's crazy-quilt feminist vision. Well, they'd all hear about it tonight.

Afterward Helen and Tretona tried to reconstruct just how the session had turned so weird, but Tretona had been in the kitchen part of the time and at one crucial juncture Helen had gone to the john with an attack of the summer squits, so the following is sketchy.

The evening started out on a very low key, the murmur of voices barely louder than the hum of the window fans. Martha Morex had been playing a fantasy game:

"Imagine a world where everything made by the boys just disappeared!" She pictured vegetable-dyed clothing drying on the grass (but no washing machines). Rhonda threw in enormous organic garden plots, marigolds deftly tucked in between the tomatoes, a natural bug barrier. "Womyn were the first farmers."

Tretona added fire-building, and getting into the swing of things, suggested that womyn must have tamed the first domestic animals while men were away hunting and making wars.

Zak reckoned that womyn must have been great inventors, devising grinding wheels, devices for weaving, and pottery techniques. "Who knows, maybe they invented knives and scrapers—for cutting cane and making huts from woven branches."

Molly waxed enthusiastic. "That's right, Zak, and then the men came home empty-handed from the hunt and grabbed the knives and that was the end of vegetarian matriarchy."

Tretona laughed but no one else did. Helen launched into an interesting story about a species of monkey that was just becoming carnivorous. Evidently only the males hunted and it appeared the females wouldn't eat meat at all.

Tretona ducked out to get more ice. When she got back Martha was carrying on about XYY chromosomal mutations and how violent men were.

Suddenly Molly, who usually didn't say much, dug a newspaper out of her backpack. "That reminds me of something I would like to share with all of you. It's a speech from a Take Back the Night march in D.C. It's in the latest issue of *Off Our Backs.*" Without even a glance up for group permission, Molly started to read. Her voice was thin and her phrasing unskilled, but the speechwriter's skill came through anyway. She wove a net of connections. Tonight we take back the streets—oppose rape—rape is violence—pornography is violence—all men are rapists—tonight we light a small candle, we give warning—tomorrow our strength will be multiplied a hundredfold, with that power we will destroy all rapists and pornographers and murderers of womynspirit.

Molly held the silence for just the right interval and then there were wild cheers as she folded up the paper. Zak was pounding the heel of her work boot. "Right on, sister, right on." Tretona waited for a pause and then spoke quietly, not daring to look at Helen.

"I'm sorry, but I really disapprove of that." Her voice shook and she faltered.

Zak spoke. Her manner was calm and nonhostile. "Maybe you'd better explain why, Tretona."

Tretona still couldn't look up. "I know it was a big pep talk to get everyone fired up for the march and stuff, but I still think that's no excuse for . . ."

No one was helping. No one understood at all. Finally Tretona got courage to lift her eyes. "Well, for one thing, it's just not true that all men are rapists. That's an awful thing to say."

Helen started to intervene, but Tretona couldn't stop now. "I know the argument. Men are the cause of patriarchy and

patriarchy legitimizes rape as a form of social control and so all
men are implicated, but that's bullshit. Let's remember what
we're talking about. Rape is forcible penetration knowing the
other person doesn't consent. My father never did that to anybody. My mother said he never even coaxed her very hard if she
wasn't in the mood. If anything he was gentle to a fault. And
my father isn't the only decent guy in the world. There are lots
of them and you all know that's true. And I don't like all that
stuff about smashing pornography. I thought we were supposed
to be against violence."

Molly was quick to reply. "Why do you always take their
side? Every time we have a discussion, Tretona, you always take
the men's side, no matter what it is."

Martha chimed in. "And you won't even read about what
patriarchy does to womyn. When we got to footbinding and
infibulation in Mary Daly you skipped that part. You admitted
last time that you hadn't read it."

Tretona answered quietly. "And I explained why I stopped
reading. And someone—I think it was Zak—said she had the
same reaction to that TV program on the Holocaust. There are
some things that are just too painful to dwell on. I think we
harden ourselves if we spend too much time contemplating pure
evil or pain. Ask any emergency room attendant, they'll tell
you."

Martha said every feminist ought to be forced to read every
chapter of Mary Daly. Tretona said that was absurd. Maybe we
should be forced to read pornography instead, since that was the
ultimate insult to women.

Helen headed for the stairs. "Hold it right there—I want to
sort this all out, but I've gotta go to the john—too much corn
on the cob. Don't anyone say anything important. . . ." She
disappeared up the staircase.

Zak asked if Helen had a touch of flu. Tretona said no, it
really was too many ripe tomatoes and maybe last night's can-
telope was off. "I'll go get her some Alka-Seltzer."

When she got back, Molly was gasping for breath and

shaking. Zak moved over to her chair immediately and Rhonda tried to hold her. "No," said Molly. "No, don't. There's nothing you can do. Nobody can do anything."

Tretona thought maybe it was the onset of an epileptic fit and tried to remember what you do about swallowed tongues. Now Molly was rocking back and forth, fists clenched down hard on her thighs. "It's everywhere—there's nothing we can do. I try and try and every day I see more."

"What's wrong, Molly?" Rhonda was shaking her.

"Patriarchy—violence against womyn. It's just destroying us all. We have to be strong, but instead we've all divided. Even womyn don't understand what's happening."

Suddenly Martha started howling. At first, Tretona thought she was just trying to distract Molly, but she was definitely off on her own trip. "Hate, hate," she cried, "there's too much hate. The men I work with—they joke about rape—they talk about fuck-or-walk parties in their pickup trucks. Meanwhile *she* laughs about pornography." Martha gestured toward Tretona. "Well, *she* doesn't have to live with it every day."

Everybody was clucking sympathetically. Jeez, thought Tretona, maybe I better get out of here. For one crazy second, a picture of Salem and women possessed by the devil flashed through her mind. Then Helen appeared and took charge. "Get ice packs," she said.

Tretona leaped at the chance to escape. When she came back Helen and Martha and Molly were all wrapped around each other. Helen jammered on and on about how a raised consciousness made one more sensitive to the injustices all around us and how healthy anger was, righteous anger that would burn and brand anyone who wouldn't listen. How from anger came power, the power to start a new society, and how important Molly and Martha and all of us were for that task. Gradually, their sobs became slower and more relaxed and then everyone was hugging except Tretona, who was holding two dish towels full of ice cubes.

Then everyone left. "Whew," said Tretona, but Helen sat

woodenly. "Here—we might as well use these ice packs."

Helen shook her head. "Tretona, I just don't see why you can't get more into the spirit of things."

"Well, I'm sorry, but when some idea is dangerous as well as absurd, I just have to say something."

"You know very well what 'all men are rapists' means. Don't you remember Jill Johnston saying that all women are lesbians? You know what she meant."

"I'm not so sure I do, as a matter of fact," said Tretona. "Anyway it's not insulting to call a woman a lesbian, but I think it's very heavy to call a man a rapist."

"But consider the effect your remarks had on Martha and Molly. They are very fragile."

"I know they are, but they're allergic to practically everything that happens in our society."

Helen's voice was clipped. "To that extent they're simply victims of patriarchy."

"Are they?" Tretona heard her own words bounce around the room. "I think they're victims of political puritanism and utopian thinking. All this group ever does is trash what there is and dream about perfect little doll houses in the big separatist sky. I think it's time we started with the here and now and started talking about alliances and working to really change things instead of trying to define perfection."

The hot humid air hung heavy between them.

"There are lots of different pathways to revolution," said Helen.

"No revolution needs people who self-destruct, women who are martyrs to their own neurasthenia," insisted Tretona. "That we can do without."

"What we can't do without is a vision," said Helen. "And sometimes it's painful even to dream. Good night." She headed up the stairs.

"Hey," said Tretona. Then as Helen paused, "Good night —sweet dreams." They both smiled at the cliché. "I mean it, Helen—*sweet* dreams. You deserve them more than anyone I know."

In the Booneville summer they had taken to separate beds, the radiant heat from another body too much to endure. Tretona longed for reassurance but dared not disturb the static status quo. Later that night a storm came, strobe lights and disco thunderbolts. Little Şeker, who feared neither snakes, geese, nor police dogs, came crawling up from the basement and burrowed between the bed and the wall. And then Helen appeared in the doorway, her naked body wrapped in a sheet. And the cooling rain bucketed down, pounding and pummeling the earth and leaving the air fresh with ozone.

At breakfast the next morning, coasting on the respite, Tretona made the announcement she had been harboring for days.

"I guess I am going to help out with the Gay Studies course. They want one of the coordinators to be a woman and I'm really the only person who can do it. Sydney goes off on leave to Oxford halfway through the semester."

Helen shrugged over her granola.

"So we may be having some planning sessions over here. It's close to campus and it isn't fair to go over to Robert's all the time."

"The place is all yours, chum. Just let me know when the gay boys are coming over so I can clear out."

Tretona dipped a bacon strip in her egg yolk and chewed ten times before answering.

"These are a pretty fine bunch of people, Helen. Gay men have some problems too, you know. And they can't hide behind a nice innocuous label like feminism."

"That's why I always say lesbian-feminist," Helen snapped.

Tretona let it pass. "By the way, when is the Midwest Womyn's Music Festival?"

Helen's quick glance scored the point. "Week after next. Tretona, you *must* go. I really want you to."

Mollified, Tretona hugged her assent, tossed the dogs their vitamin pills, and headed off to her office whistling.

7.

Music and The Ruffled Breast

August is country-fair time in the midwest. Farm families load up the 4-H animals and prize rutabagas and head for the fairgrounds, first the county and then, if you are lucky, on to the state capital. It's a great time for gossiping and catching up on the latest pest control and trouble-free balers. City folks come too. They pet the 1,000-pound calves, cheer madly for Dolly Parton or Willie Nelson, and laugh good-naturedly at the rodeo clowns.

Little kids scurry around like guerrilla soldiers, sneaking off from their duties in the 4-H tent to blow a whole summer's allowance on rides and cotton candy and shooting galleries. Tretona remembered the agony of choosing between the Octopus and the Dodge-em Cars. And the excitement of broken-field running through the Midway crowd, scrupulously avoiding all parents, especially your own—unless you were out of money and wanted to wheedle an advance. Little clumps of kids milling about, discussing which operator gave you the longest ride. Listening spellbound to the shill outside the Freak Show, wondering if there really was a two-headed calf and a hermaphrodite inside. And the Geek who swallowed snakes alive! What kind of human being would do such a disgusting thing? But then all carnival people were pretty exotic. One year there was a boy her own age who was helping out on the Bullet. Tretona kept staring at him—he wore a black vest with studs. No shirt. Hair dirty blond and down over his ears at a time when all the country kids had burr haircuts. Feeling safe because there was a fence between them, Tretona even asked him a couple of questions. Did the Bullet have a reverse gear? Did he go to school in the winter? No, to both questions—it didn't need one and he had already finished eighth grade. In a way, not going to high school was more shocking to Tretona's sensibilities than swallowing snakes. It convinced her that carnival people were descended from gypsies and were strange and possibly dangerous.

Now, thirty years later, she was on her way to an Amazon Fair—a gathering of strange, exotic, and dangerous womyn! Right this very minute, she thought, 8,000 lesbians from all over the country were leaping into tin lezzies and all heading for seventeen acres somewhere in the Michigan woods. Eight thousand! A couple of years ago she wouldn't have believed that there were that many in the whole history of the world.

"I just can't imagine eight thousand dykes all together in one place," she said to Zak, who was driving.

"It is pretty incredible, no doubt about it." Zak expertly lit a cigarette while passing a semi. "Sometimes the energy level is so high the air almost shimmers. Like last year it had been raining for three days. (Hope you remembered to bring a poncho. The weather can be miserable.) Anyway we were all cold and wet sitting on the ground listening to Holly Near and shivering. Then she got us all singing and everyone cheered up. And then suddenly the clouds rolled back and the moon came up over the hill behind us and Holly pointed to it and everyone turned to look. And then it was like everyone levitated and we were all howling and laughing and hugging. And the Alive band started drumming and an enormous snake dance formed and we congoed all over the camp and picked up the kitchen workers and all ended up back in the amphitheatre and we must have sung 'Filling Up and Spilling Over' at least fifty times. No one could stop. The festival is all just so incredible. I never went to Woodstock but I'm sure this is a thousand times more wonderful."

"Eight thousand times." Tretona couldn't get over the sheer quantity. Secretly she was a little worried about 8,000 dykes all peeing in the woods and showing up late for K.P.—she'd packed some Lomotil and Halazone tablets just in case. However, Helen swore the festival was very well organized. "And the public health inspectors come every fucking day. The announcement always goes out: 'Shirts on for the boys in blue!' They provide them with an escort of karate black belts."

"To keep them from harassing the womyn?" Tretona asked.

"Hell, no. To protect them from eight thousand revved-up angry Amazons who don't want any boys telling them what is or isn't healthy. So far there hasn't been any incident."

Tretona sought out Helen now in the back of the RV. Zak's stepfather had a ludicrously big ecological disaster that he used for vacations and also as a traveling exhibit room for his aluminum-siding business. Zak was amazed when he offered to loan it for the Michigan trip. He didn't even blink when the whole lot of them drove over to pick it up.

"Have fun at the fair, girls," he boomed. "And if anyone wants some siding or storm windows, give them my card. There's a whole boxfull in the dash."

At the first gas stop, though, the RV was redecorated with BonAmi graffiti: "Booneville Amazons" went on the back window. And next to the Uncle Sam poster exhorting us to conserve energy with aluminum storm doors, someone added "Good Dykes make Good Neighbors" and "Les-Be Friends." It was going to be a great trip, OK.

Tretona staggered from the navigator's seat up by Zak all the way back to the rear bench where Helen was lounging against a rolled-up sleeping bag. Together they watched the glacier-flat fields of northern Indiana unrolling in the dusk. Suddenly Tretona burst into song. "One of these days I'm gonna take a vacation. . . ." She squeezed Helen's ankles. "Boy—this is just what I deserve—four whole days away from that fucking office. I'm not going to do nothing but soak up fresh air and listen to music."

Helen smiled back. "Actually this is the busiest time of the year for me."

"God, Helen. Don't tell me you try to organize the kitchen staff or something."

"Tretona, will you stop worrying about getting fed? The Music Collective has everything wonderfully under control. No, I do networking, connecting with old friends. Lots of interchange. Like I must talk to Marty Flye—about her essay on degrees of separatism. I think as abstract analysis it is viable, but not as a basis for action—it's too susceptible to compromise. And someone said that this year Bernie Tennenborn was going to be here—she's done very good work on feminist aesthetics, but here again I think there's a descriptive/normative conflict. . . ."

Tretona's attention flagged and she half smiled, thinking how similar Helen sounded to any establishment academician en route to a professional conference. But hark!

". . . vaginal landscapes—I think that's what she called them. She started out doing closeups of lips. Have you ever seen a ten-by-thirteen blow-up of lips? The little cracks and the tip of the tongue and stuff—it's all very interesting. Then for a while she photographed body contours, mostly breasts and swatches of buttocks in soft focus—you really couldn't tell what it was. Anyway, she said in her solstice letter that she had a new macro lens and floodlights rigged up in her camper so she could do vaginal landscapes at the Music Festival. That's Irmgard for you! She'll have a line outside her tent about a mile long."

Wow, this *is* really like an academic convention, thought Tretona, complete with the obligatory slut down the hall. "Is Irmgard German or Scandinavian?" she asked.

"Pure California, as far as I know," answered Helen. "But very exotic—and a creator of feminist erotica. Hey, I hope you aren't getting the wrong idea. Irmgard's photos are very revolutionary and womyn-affirming. What she does in her art is to force us to really look at our own bodies and to come to terms with them. It's just that she uses a lens instead of a speculum.

You'll like her—she's kind of a scientist-artist-philosopher all rolled into one."

For a split second Tretona wondered if Helen was trying to fix her up with Irmgard—while Helen herself did what? It was strange. Here Helen was, a card-carrying nonmonogamist if there ever was one, and yet as far as Tretona could tell she never looked at anyone else. Still, the knowledge that Helen might pop off somewhere, leave town even, left Tretona feeling—not exactly suspicious, more like hollow and edgy. It was crazy really. It was totally impractical to make an irreversible commitment—every book on decision theory would give you a million reasons against it: the external situation might change, one's preference rankings were labile, something better might come along. All in all, mixed strategies with lots of options left open were definitely called for.

Yet somewhere inside her there was a longing for vows, for some kind of permanency and long-term planning. Was this a patriarchal leftover, or just an adolescent romantic hang-up?

Tretona sighed. Why couldn't she be civilized and sensible like Helen? Except that Helen's cool always seemed a little like veneer. Granted it hadn't cracked yet, but if it ever did, Tretona wasn't at all sure what would emerge. Never mind, they were off on a wonderful holiday excursion. And hadn't Helen gone out of her way to invite her?

The clocks in Indiana run on God's time, by gum, so they lost an hour when they crossed the Michigan state line. The RV had started out on Dyke Standard Time of course and what with endless stops for gas, MacDonald's, insect repellent, cherries from a roadside stand, and cigarette papers it was well past midnight when Zak negotiated the last faintly marked turn onto the narrow gravel road and pulled up at a saw-horse barrier. Over to the left was a campfire and three womyn with flashlights soon appeared. One carried a clipboard and immediately started writing down the license number.

"Let's see your passes," said the tall one in overalls.

"Hey, we just got here," said Zak. "We haven't registered yet."

"OK. We'll fix you up. Sorry to be so rude, but we've had some local rednecks in a four-wheeler driving around out here and when I saw whatever-this-thing-is I thought maybe they'd come back in a tank."

"Well there *are* eight of us, but we are friendly invaders," Zak replied.

The third guardian of the gate poked her head in the passenger window. "Have you any dogs or male children over six?"

"No—eight adults." It seemed agreed that Zak would do all the talking.

After they had "cleared customs" and paid for their tickets Tretona queried Helen in a low voice: "What was that bit about dogs and children?"

"Well, dogs aren't allowed. You can't have eight thousand pooches milling around; maybe more than eight thousand. After all, you've got three!"

"But kids? Can't children come?" (What happened to the whole big deal about child care, Tretona wondered.)

Helen's voice shifted into that super-reasonable tone—the way dental assistants talk right before you get massacred.

"Well, boys over six aren't allowed on the grounds. They stay at a separate camp down the road."

Molly chimed in, "It's quite a ways down the road—seven miles actually. But there's a shuttle service that goes out there several times a day."

"And there's twenty-four-hour child care," Helen added. "Some of the mothers stay here in camp so they're close to the concerts and just go out to visit."

Tretona was getting the picture. "And what if someone has two kids, a boy and a girl? Makes it kind of rough, doesn't it? But I suppose we all have to make sacrifices in the struggle for equality."

Helen did not reply. The RV lurched along the dirt lane. Bouncing past the back windows were the silhouettes of tents and the occasional gas lantern or campfire. Zak found a spot to her liking and expertly inched the big van back between two trees. "Welcome to Michigan!" she shouted and turned off the ignition. In the ensuing commotion Helen grabbed Tretona's arm and forced her to remain seated.

"Listen, you wise-ass. Womyn have been systematically excluded from government, from commerce, from religious ceremonies for thousands of years. You've experienced it—remember your stories about what farm women couldn't do and about being kept out of the senior common rooms in England? I've experienced it. We've all experienced it. So if for four days out of the year womyn want to leave our rotten sexist society and camp out in the woods by themselves, I don't think any bleeding heart liberal should object. Understand?"

"I understand, Helen. But I wonder if these little boys understand. The cycle has to stop somewhere."

The commotion of eight people scrambling for sleeping bags made further debate impossible. And when everything was finally squared away Helen had disappeared.

"She probably went to the latrine," Zak said.

Embarrassed to be so obviously waiting, Tretona moved her pallet outside. In any case, the RV was parked on a slant and it was crowded inside. The grass was sopping wet with dew so she dug out a poncho. It was too cold for mosquitoes, but just in case she fastened a net onto a bumper guard and draped it over the little inflatable pillow she had had since Girl Scout days.

Somehow she had unconsciously thought the festival would be sort of like summer camp—lots of songs about rotten peanuts and pruney faces, everyone keen on fire-building and proper bedrolls. But it wasn't like that at all. Whatever was going on here was much more intense—and much more anarchistic. For a moment Tretona thought of moving everything back inside. What if Zak started up the motor or someone pulled in alongside and ran over her legs? But then it suddenly occurred to her—the crucial difference between this gathering of Amazons and a Girl Scout Round-up was sexual freedom. Here young women held hands and lay in each other's arms without fear or guilt. With a flash of desire and embarrassment Tretona remembered her summer-long seduction of Sparky, an exchange counselor from Austria—the times they deliberately got lost on canoe trips, their conniving to share puptents on overnights, the near misses when campers burst into the staff lounge unexpectedly, and, alas, Tretona's phony arguments to the effect that she and Sparky's boyfriend back home were not competitors. "It's not a question of who's to be first violin—we play entirely different instruments."

Tretona sighed. Maybe all that training in sophistry was part of the reason she had become a philosopher. At least the years of hypocrisy and outright lies were over, especially now that she was with Helen—who, by the way, ought to be back by now. Dare she move her sleeping bag out too so as not to disturb the others? No—too pushy. Let her do her own thing.

But although determined not to wait up for Helen (which state of mind generally guarantees insomnia), Tretona soon fell fast asleep.

* * *

Wakened by a blast of sunshine, Tretona pulled on shorts and sweatshirt and bounced into the RV. She grabbed a canteen from the snore-filled gloomy interior and headed toward what she hoped was the center of the camp.

The atmosphere was that of a medieval fair. There were tents everywhere, pitched helter-skelter amidst heavy ferns and scruffy pine trees. An enormous teepee covered with bear footprints dominated one hillock. Nearby a lavender banner announced the Womyn of Wichita Wicca. Three dykes in leather jackets slept *à la belle étoile* next to an enormous Harley.

People were beginning to stir and, coming around a bend, Tretona almost ran into a coffee pot perched precariously over a tiny fire. The cook apologized for being in the road, Tretona apologized for walking over the speed limit, and then they exchanged grins and hometowns: Booneville, Indiana; Guelph, Ontario.

Oh! it really is an international conference. Well, Pan American at least—some folk from Mexico over there. We almost didn't make it through customs. Really? What was the problem? They knew we were coming *here*. Really?

As usual Tretona felt embarrassed when her country screwed up. Even after the Bomb and Vietnam and the opposition to the ERA, she still had some residual patriotism.

Anyway, I'm glad you got through OK. Oh sure, no problem—we wouldn't let a couple of tin badges keep us away from the festival. It's the world's longest unguarded border, you know. More grins and quiet byes.

And so Tretona floated through a sea of gentleness and warm small talk. Canteens passed around to fill tooth mugs, communal soap at the cold showers. There was a bit of a scramble for blueberries, but in general the food queues were relaxed and orderly. Tretona loaded up more granola, yogurt, and peanut butter than she really wanted but didn't dare waste any.

The morning was half gone before she saw any of the gang she had come up with. Zak was wearing cut-off bib overalls with no shirt.

"Hey, Tiger. Pretty cute outfit."

"You like it? It's my new frock for the festival."

"You seen Helen?"

"Naw. She's around someplace I expect."

And so Tretona drifted through the Merchant's tent and bought a small copper labrys that she pinned on her Lacoste T-shirt (she'd cut off the alligator just before coming, but the stitches still showed). Past the outdoor hairdressers. One woman was getting what looked like a Mohawk—someone else was having her thick blond hair plaited into cornrows. Under the next tree was a body-painting salon.

Jewlery, perm, manicure? This *is* a woman's festival! The idea reinforced by a tapestry and embroidery display. Tretona stopped under a tent where a workshop was underway. The group silent and staring as she entered. Then, "This session is for Armenian lesbians."

"Oh, sorry," stumbling out. Better find a program. Off past the Womb Health tent—two doors, one labeled Herbal Healing, the other simply marked First Aid. Over the hill and there at eye level was a naked woman's belly—upside down. The arms were crossed and her face beet red. The human pendulum was wearing enormous ski boots fastened to a board which in turn was suspended by a pulley cable arrangement fastened to a tree branch.

Tretona's imagination failed her completely. There was a small circle of silent onlookers. An older woman in a madras dress took pity on her bewilderment. "Indian chiropractic," she whispered.

Tretona nodded and stumbled down the hill. The familiar sight of dykes playing volleyball was reassuring and one of the other spectators even had a program. Let's see—Womyn on the Land, Small Presses, Art and Survival, Tai Chi—ah, here we go: The Politics of Pornography. She even knew the workshop location—the auxiliary day performers' stage over by the food lines. The discussion was already in full swing when Tretona arrived. Tired from her morning's rambles, she picked her way around the folks sitting on the ground and got a place in front where she could lean against the stage.

". . . and in pornography we find patriarchal society's attitude toward womyn writ large. Women are objects, fucking machines, orifices, receptacles for cocks—that's in soft porn. But what really sells are womyn scourged by whips and chains, torn flesh and complete degradation—that's what men pay to see."

The speaker's voice was firm and matter-of-fact. Another woman chimed in. "Some people will try to tell you it's just fantasy material, that it doesn't affect behavior. Well, I was married to a man who was into pornography and I'm here to tell you it does matter. He was always trying to get me to go to X-rated movies—he said I needed loosening up. Well, one night I went with him just to shut him up, besides it was Japanese and

I thought it couldn't be too bad. Well, it was *In the Realm of the Senses*—have you heard about it? And when we got home, he threw me down in front of the fireplace and laid a poker across my throat with both hands and started to rape me and strangle me at the same time."

Her voice shook and the womyn nearby formed a comforting shelter as the speaker continued:

"I couldn't scream or anything. I might not be alive today if Greta, our big German police dog, hadn't come in."

"Did she attack him?"

"Hell, no. She thought we were wrestling and got right in the middle and started licking Josh's face. The bastard started giggling and lost his erection. I could hardly speak when I got up. But I remember gasping out, 'Looks like you needed a double feature.' And then I called Greta and took her with me to the Battered Woman's Shelter and they gave her a whole pound of hamburger as a reward. I never will forget sitting in the kitchen with an ice pack on my throat watching Greta eating that hamburger. I think she saved my life."

The woman was silent, so silent that those around her stopped their soothing and swaying. There was a gap and then someone far over on the other side spoke in a voice so deep and vibrant that everyone craned to see the source.

"Pornography consists of images, of words, of ideas. If successful, these images evoke sexual responses and sexual responses are very powerful. Our sister has just described a very ugly and cruel response. But pornography can be liberating too."

The assemblage buzzed defensively like a hive of angry bees but the voice projected through the grumble.

"Lady Chatterly's Lover, Ulysses, The Well of Loneliness—each of those books moved me, changed my life, yet each was legally indicted as pornography."

There were shouted objections: "Those books aren't what we're talking about. They were just out to get Radclyffe Hall because she was a dyke."

Tretona found herself on her feet. "But that's just her point. As soon as you start limiting freedom of expression, then the majority, those good burghers, think they can define what community standards ought to be. They can go after any sort of sexual expression that doesn't fit into their little missionary manuals." Tretona's adrenalin level flattened out. "Or at least I think that's what she meant, that person over there. . . ."

"My name's Irmgard," said Velvet Voice. "I'll even stand up for tacky porn, not just the classics. When I was a teenager and not out yet, I used to go buy smokes in a tavern that had a girlie calendar just so I could ogle those overendowed ladies in black lace. And maybe I was more retarded than the rest of you but I never knew what dykes did in bed—I really didn't—until I found one of my brother's magazines with two womyn going at it. They must have been dykes—I fell in love with both of them. In fact if either one is here, please hunt me up afterward. Of course, at the end a big dick came and finished them off, but I tore that page out."

The tall dark woman who had been talking when Tretona arrived interjected, "Irmgard, we're not talking about teenage masturbation, we're talking about violence—sexual violence against womyn, like this poor woman endured. It *has* to stop—and the only way to stop it is to get rid of pornography."

Irmgard's voice became very deep. "It's not that easy, Drina. I saw *Realm of the Senses* too. I thought it was a very beautiful movie, very provocative, very well done. I didn't go home and rape or strangle anyone. I'm sorry someone's husband did, but *he* has to bear responsibility for that, not the movie. It's *behavior* that has to be controlled, not art, and that even includes tacky exploitative art, because I don't trust any censor to do my discriminating for me."

Drina jumped up on the platform. "Any womyn who are tired of First Amendment bullshit and want to plan collective action against pornography, are invited to join me in the grove over by the showers in five minutes."

There were shouts of approval, a few protests of "Why

should *we* have to leave?" and then a general exodus.

Tretona, not quite knowing what to do, stayed by the platform, trying to look inconspicuous. Suddenly, standing beside her were two butter-brown legs extending from the shortest cut-offs she had ever seen, topped off by a maroon lace smock.

"Well, we sure chased them off, didn't we!" It was Irmgard, smiling, her hand on one hip.

Tretona jumped to her feet, apologetic. "I'm sorry the meeting broke up, but I thought you were absolutely right to . . ."

Irmgard flashed her a big smile. "Don't worry your head. Drina likes nothing better than making a dramatic exit. She did the same thing at a WAP meeting when I tried to compromise by drawing a distinction between the erotic and the pornographic. That's why I launched a frontal assault this time. She and her droogs are probably over there ranting away now, pleased as punch to be martyrs in exile."

Tretona still looked concerned. "You'll have to admit that was a pretty moving story about the woman getting strangled. It took some courage to talk about it."

"Are you kidding? That little wimp's got her performance down pat. She's with a speakers' bureau in Minneapolis and tells that story everywhere she goes. You'd think it was the only thing significant that ever happened to her." Irmgard's brown braids bounced in a thick coil on the back of her head.

Tretona persisted. "Still, it's a true story and one that's worth telling."

Irmgard softened. "You're right, but she's so damned self-indulgent about it."

There was a silence. Then Irmgard suggested a walk out to the Lookout Point. "Afterward if you like, I can even give you lunch down at the camper. Yogurt and brown rice twice a day is too much."

They ambled past a pair of jugglers; breasts flashed as they tossed pins back and forth. A woman with vines woven into her Medusa-like hair sat on a stump engrossed in her own guitar playing.

Tretona was still thinking about the raped woman. "You said she was self-indulgent. What's the difference between that and the kind of personal story-telling and sharing experiences that is the hallmark of feminist groups? Or do you think it's all just narcissistic moaning?"

"No," said Irmgard. "Let me think, maybe I saw too many stoic cowboy movies when I was a kid. Wait, I'll tell you a story that will help explain—"

The Story of Mrs. Klappholz's Tattoo as told by Irmgard.

Mr. and Mrs. Klappholz lived next door to us in Oakland. They were always friendly enough in a formal sort of way. I must have been ten or so when they moved in. I used to talk to Mrs. Klappholz when she was working on her flower boxes and then I'd come home and mimic her accent.

Most of the time she wore long-sleeved dresses. They were all cut from the same pattern, but she had made them up out of all sorts of different fabrics, always in dull muted colors, though.

Slowly I got to know her better and once in a while I was invited in. One Memorial Day I was over there—I remember that my folks had gone to the cemetery—and Mrs. Klappholz was baking bread and had her sleeves rolled up. There on her left arm were some blue numbers. I kept staring at them and finally I asked what they were.

Mrs. Klappholz just kept kneading the bread and didn't say anything. Mr. Klappholz was in the living room in his chair rocking and looking at the flower boxes. "Mutti," he said. "Our guest asked you a question."

"She's too young," said Mrs. Klappholz. Well, you can imagine that I was really curious then.

"No I'm not too young," I insisted. "Why'd you get a tattoo?"

"I was in a concentration camp," she said.

My first reaction was embarrassment and it must have been obvious because she reached over and patted me—I remember it was with the tattooed arm—and said, "Don't fret, dear. I'll explain when you're a little older."

My mother filled me in on the Holocaust and said not to pester Mrs. Klappholz for details because she probably didn't want to think about it.

I tried to be extra thoughtful from then on and didn't chalk up her sidewalk with hopscotch squares because I figured she didn't like to scrub them off and she always gave me a new notebook in the fall and asked to see my report card.

I must have gradually forgotten about the tattoo—maybe she kept her sleeve down—for at first I didn't know what she was referring to when she gave me a present on my sixteenth birthday.

"You know when you asked about my numbers? Now you are grown up. You can even drive a car, yes? So, you can understand this book." And then she gave me an abridged edition of *Mein Kampf!*

Well, my father was shocked. He just couldn't understand why a survivor of the camps would give a sweet young girl a book by Adolf Hitler. He sort of hinted that I should shelve it and make polite noises if she should ever mention it again. But my mom said—I remember how sad her voice was: "You should read a little of it, Irma. Every generation has to fight fascism in some form or another."

A three-hundred-foot climb is a great achievement on a midwestern summer day. Tretona mopped her brow with her shirttail and wished she'd worn a straw hat. Together they surveyed the festival grounds. Work crews were still messing with the lights and sound equipment for the big stage. Already people were reserving ground space for the evening's concert—the natural amphitheatre was quilted with blankets, ponchos, and picnic coolers. Womyn dotted the landscape like wildflowers, clustering around cool, wooded centers and forming a sensuous winding chain around the food tables.

"Eight thousand dykes," sighed Tretona.

"All looking for happiness, respect, and freedom." Irmgard seemed pensive. "I just wish they'd realize how important tolerance is if we're to get any of those good things."

"Of each other?" asked Tretona.

"I mean of everybody," came the reply.

Tretona took hold of her arm and then didn't know what to do next. "Hey, what about lunch? I'm very tolerant of home cooking."

* * *

Tretona circled the amphitheatre looking for Helen. It was probably a hopeless task. She tried vainly to remember all those
random walk calculations from thermodynamics. But the im-
probable does happen, frequently, as a matter of fact. Suddenly
Tretona felt a tug at her shorts and there, right behind her, were
Zak, Molly, *and Helen!*

"Where you been all day?"

Tretona was flustered and blurted out: "Where were you all
night?"

Molly and Zak busied themselves with the backpacks.

"I was at a campfire—we stayed up all night confronting
our own racism—it was wonderful—I mean it was awful to
think about how much racism there is—but it was good to start
working on it."

"Oh," said Tretona.

"Here, I brought your sweatpants. Put 'em on. You freeze
when it gets dark. You're sunburned, aren't you? Here, have a
granola bar."

Ever mollified by mothering and goodies, Tretona sank
down on the ground cloth. "Wow, you've even got canoe
chairs!"

Zak beamed. "There's room for everything in an RV."

Now that she was tucked in and munching with Helen's
arms on her knee, Tretona gazed contentedly at the dykes milling around and settling in for the concert. No wonder social
scientists go mad when they try to make up generalizations
about queers, she thought. In the 120 degrees she could scan
without moving her head there were: a Miss Wyoming looka-
like wearing a silver Danskin leotard, a 250-pound woman
wearing a man's undershirt and smoking a pipe, a half-naked
Greek goddess with flowers plaited all over her head, a statu-
esque black woman in a white tux messing with the stage mike,
two toughies shoving each other (it was a dispute about the
boundaries of the chemically free zone—security women with
orange armbands quickly broke it up). There were little kids
(girl kids) with Indian-painted faces, a beaming old woman with

a Sierra Club tin cup tied to her waist, lots of anti-nuke T-shirts, but someone in a cowboy hat was wearing an American flag.

We all share a common oppression, Tretona thought. That's good enough for political action but hardly the basis for community.

The mike crackled. "Good evening, all you lovely dykes!" A roar of approval. "Kiss the womyn sitting next to you—" Giggles. "Go on." Confused hugs. "Did you check to see if she had grease under her fingernails?" Absolute shrieks. "Well, if she did, please send her right over to the Transport tent. Rubyfruit is having some ignition problems, but I'm sure if someone with a little knowhow will just twiddle with her plugs—she has *eight* of them you know." Laughter building to applause.

No, it's more than just oppression, mused Tretona. We have our own humor and our own literature and—as the first group struck up—and, most of all, our own Music!

8.

Reentry Problems

It was with considerable relief that Tretona finally closed the door of the RV. Precisely fifty-five minutes late, she noted. Oh hell, that was pretty good really. She tried to tune into the vehicular mood.

Nostalgia had already set in and there were dreamy-eyed plans for next year. "Let's come up on Wednesday and help put up the tents." "I hear that next year Meg Christian will come for sure?" "Ooh—did you know I talked to Evelyn for a real long time." "Who's that?" "Evelyn? Are you kidding? She's that real neat womyn in Sweet Honey of the Rock. You remember the tall one, kind of thin, with the green top on?" "Well, I think Bernice is just amazing. When she led that chantlike song . . ."

Well, I vote for Ringo, thought Tretona. Paul and George are out in front but Ringo is so cool. Jeez, groupies are dumb, no matter *who* the group is. She looked to Helen for some sign of shared skepticism, but Helen was preening her consciousness. "Tretona, we must explore this whole issue of racism in the Ovular. I can't believe how insensitive we've been."

"How's that?" said Tretona.

"Well, what could be more racist than our selection of books? Not a single one by a womyn of color. No wonder no Third World womyn come."

"I'm not sure how many foreign students are dykes," said Tretona. "I suppose some of them are, but it's kind of diffi-cult . . ."

"No, I mean Americans," snapped Helen. "Who's that black womyn you talk to down at Bullwinkles?"

"Diane Johnson? Sure, I know her. She played second base. Sure, I can invite her and her lover—I think her name is Janetta."

"Good, that's a start. We must overcome our own racism." Helen was moving on down the list on her mental clipboard. "And I think the Ovulars should be chemically free. What do you think? The living room is too small to partition." Tretona tried to remember if Diane smoked. That would be just great— invite her over and then make her sit out in the kitchen.

"Well, we'd better not light the fireplace then," said Tretona.

Helen looked up quizzically.

"Because, sometimes it smokes."

Helen ignored the remark and pursued her agenda. "And we need to do some more language awareness, too."

Tretona waited to hear what word was going to get the X-chromosome axe this time—*human, history, poetess, seminal* had already been zapped. Maybe *menstruation?*

"Fat chance. Fat lip," said Helen. "Expressions like that are really patriarchy's way of excluding people."

But what about *the fatted calf?* thought Tretona. Of course, it was for the prodigal son, so that won't work. It was no use resisting Helen anyway. Her brand of philology plus free association plus righteous indignation was not to be argued with.

"Rest stop!" announced Zak and pulled into the Hoosier Hills auto plaza.

Unwilling to compete with seven dykes and two women with beehive hairdos for the single toilet stall, Tretona drifted around the corner and wandered past the hydraulic lift into the Men's Room. It was a trick she'd learned when whole busloads of Girl Scouts stopped en route to camp.

The cubicle smelled of wine and Lava soap and there was no seat on the toilet, but it was better than waiting. She squatted over the porcelain bowl and idly read the graffiti—cruder and

less romantic than the linked initials or even occasional paeans
to cocks that were standard fare among the Powder Room set.
What was this?

"Why shouldn't nigger babies play in sand piles?" demanded someone with a fiber pen. "'Cause the cats might cover
them up," came the answer.

Tretona didn't get it at first. Then she almost smiled before
feelings of disgust and anger took over. "Jeez, I guess Helen is
right," she thought. "Anyone who grows up in a racist society
gets tarred by the brush." Then she wondered if it was objectionable to use *tarred* in that way.

Slowly she flushed the toilet and then rubbed a Kleenex in
the soap and scrubbed off the sand pile story, but left the pictures of dripping cocks intact. There was a limit to what one
person could clean up. A mechanic looked at her a little weird
as she walked out but didn't say anything.

Still, she thought, there are degrees. It's one thing to smile
a little at a stupid joke and quite another to lynch somebody.
It's one thing not to go out of your way to invite certain people
to your parties and quite another to not let them vote or refuse
to give them a job. That's what Helen just couldn't accept: that
there are degrees. And it seemed like she'd get just as self-
righteous over a flubbed pronoun as over a rape. Tretona had a
painful memory of old Mrs. Zillard, her first-grade teacher, who
hollered at her for folding an arithmetic paper the wrong way
even though all the sums were correct.

Nobody was back at the RV yet so Tretona wandered
across the parking lot to the little grocery and souvenir store.
What was that horse and buggy doing there? For a moment she
thought it was an advertising gimmick but then she noticed the
little Amish boy tending the horses. He was wearing a black suit
with the shirt buttoned up all the way and his pant legs were
stuffed into rubber boots.

"Nice-looking team you got there," said Tretona. The boy
stared at her but his face was expressionless. Maybe he doesn't
understand English, she thought.

"Schönes Wetter, heute," she tried tentatively, but the boy looked away.

The rest of the family was inside, though that couldn't be all of them. Tretona pretended to be reading a recipe on an oatmeal box so she could stare at them. Mama and Daughter both wore navy blue sunbonnets and long cloaks. Papa had a remarkable gray beard. They seemed to be deciding which size container of Lysol to buy. The woman's face was pale as an angel's but when she reached out to take the bottle Tretona could see how brown and gnarled her hands were.

The group moved on with unhurried stride and silently paid for their purchases.

Keep the faith, baby, Tretona thought. The papers in Booneville were always reporting legal hassles with the Amish. For example, all farm vehicles were supposed to bear a triangular warning sign, but to the Amish it was a symbol of the devil.

Tretona walked back out to see if this buggy had one. When the father ordered the horses to back up Tretona noticed how rotten his teeth were. They pulled away—sure enough no warning sign—and just for a moment the boy looked back at her.

I bet the Amish used to be revolutionaries, thought Tretona. I bet they came over here pure and enthusiastic and built big barns and thought everyone would see how great their lifestyle was. And now they're just an anachronism; all they've got is their closed little community with beautiful horses and rotten teeth. Would the Lesbian Nation fare any better?

"Hi, Cutie!" Tretona whirled around and then fell in with Zak and the others. After four days of yogurt and salt-free peanut butter, everyone was ready for junk food. Like locusts —no, more like army ants—they tore into Doritos, Cokes, pickles, and packets of beef jerky. One kind of bubble gum even had pictures of women athletes on it, so between them they stripped the rack of Billie Jean Kings and Babe Zaharias.

They whooped it up and horsed around in the checkout line and all the way back to the van. Tretona's mood improved enormously and she even managed to turn a cartwheel holding a bag of snacks in her teeth. Which produced great cheers and a flurry of leapfrogging.

"Oh my God!" Zak sounded like someone had kicked the wind out of her.

"What's wrong?" Martha asked. Zak just pointed dumbly at a car.

Typical Chevy wedding regalia: tin cans, crepe-paper streamers, "Just Married" scrawled in whitewash. The trunk sported a home-made billboard:

"She got Him today, but He'll get Her tonight."

Martha finally broke the silence. "Ooh—that's really gross." Somehow they all looked over at Helen. Tretona half expected an impromptu lecture in front of this epitome of patriarchy, but Helen didn't do anything.

"Let's turn the fucking car over," growled Zak.

"No, no, don't," said Tretona, more worried that it was too heavy and that they wouldn't succeed than afraid of being caught.

"Well, let's at least cut that sign down," said Martha, searching vainly for a pocket knife. Zak helpfully offered a pair of nail clippers. Then they all looked at Helen again.

Helen pursed her lips and then slowly, dramatically, she blew an enormous bubble. It shimmered for a moment in sun, then turned flaccid and withdrew back into Helen's mouth.

They all piled back into the RV. Tretona opened her Doritos. At first they tasted a little stale, but she ate the whole bag and licked out the seams.

9.

Sistercraft Is Powerful

New Year's Day comes on August 27 or thereabouts in Booneville, Indiana. All summer long it's a sleepy little town, the only excitement provided by the detour on Third Street when the city fixes potholes or the occasional arrest of kids swimming at the quarries. And then suddenly it's Registration Week and 5,000 freshmen drive into town and unpack their 5,000 record players, and wander around looking for classrooms, lovers, and the meaning of life. Booneville merchants happily ring away on their cash registers while SIU professors gloomily shelve unfinished research and resolve to get more done next summer. Ready for it or not, the New Year has begun.

The Gay Studies committee had just missed the deadline for the approval of new courses. Not wanting to give anyone an excuse for rejecting it, they decided to postpone their application until the spring. As a consequence Tretona didn't have an overload and hence didn't have any excuse when the chairman approached her about giving a series of guest lectures in what they all called "The Marijuana Course."

Darwin Frazier was not exactly your typical charismatic teacher. He ran his huge lecture courses like he ran departmental meetings—calmly, systematically, with tedious care for every detail. His father had evidently been a big popular professional atheist (hence the "Darwin") who ran around debating preachers and calling on God to come out of the clouds and strike him dead if He was so damn powerful. Son Frazier also tried to deal with controversial topics, but if he ever won arguments it was by boring the audience to death. Still, the undergraduates flocked into his class on Practical Reasoning. Some said it was because he used research on marijuana as a case study. Others reckoned it was a gut course. Whatever the reason for it, its size kept the department afloat by providing money for extra graduate assistants.

"What exactly did you want me to lecture on?" asked Tretona. Actually, that was a bad gambit. If he mentioned a topic she didn't know much about, that would make her look bad; but if it were something familiar, then she'd be stuck and have to do it.

"Oh, something on the occult—witchcraft, alchemy, astrology—whatever you like. I thought a little pseudoscience would contrast nicely with the *science* that I'll teach them later." Frazier looked pleased with the prospects.

You smug son-of-a-bitch, thought Tretona. I'm supposed to hold up the straw man so you can demolish it? For a moment she contemplated lecturing on the *similarities* between science and the so-called pseudosciences: alchemists did experiments, while nothing is more occult than modern particle physics. But that was a no-win strategy. If she succeeded too well in dramatizing the similarities, Frazier would crap himself and accuse her of obscurantism. And if she tried and didn't succeed, Frazier would spend the rest of the semester chortling away, "Despite Dr. Getroek's valiant defense, I think we all fully realize the intellectual poverty of the pseudosciences . . ." No, the only solution was to do both sides of the dialectic herself. She put on her best pre-tenure smile.

"That's an intriguing possibility, Darwin. How many lectures were you thinking of?"

"Oh, three, four, as many as you like really. It takes a little while to get used to the amphitheatre in the Chemistry building."

So that was it. Probably item #29a on somebody's tenure

checklist: candidate's performance in large classroom teaching situations.

But in the end Tretona really got into preparing the lectures. She made up slides of all sorts of sexy alchemical symbols —hermaphroditic glassware with androgynous figures traced out in the fumes. She dug out Paracelsus' views on syphilis and related them to his alchemical beliefs about mercury. For the astrology unit she did a lot of work on her own horoscope—it might come in handy at a party sometime. She hunted up the passage in Plato where he describes the twelve types of character needed for an ideal state and related them to the astrological signs. Frazier would like the classical allusion.

And sure enough her delivery did improve as she got used to the microphone cord trailing around underfoot and the damn motorized blackboards whose switches seemed to be wired up backwards. Then there was the distraction of two hundred and fifty pairs of staring eyes and shuffling feet.

By the end of the third lecture she was happily booming away. "So we see that many of the questions that intrigued alchemists and astrologers *are* amenable to scientific investigation—they have been or are being answered by modern chemistry, medicine, astronomy, psychology. However, the *methods* that these early thinkers used were not scientific. For example, they had no conception of a controlled experiment—Dr. Frazier will undoubtedly tell you all about controlled experiments later in the course." (Frazier nodded vigorously.)

"But there's something even more important than the experimental method." (Frazier looked worried.) "And that is the critical spirit. Paracelsus was *very* critical of Aristotle and Galen, very critical." (Tretona paused, wondering if she should say anything about his burning up all the traditional medical books in the town square, but decided against it.)

"And Plato is a good example of how we should not only criticize other people's ideas but also welcome criticism of our own. Plato taught his pupils to criticize him, just as his teacher, Socrates, had taught him to be critical.

"The early practitioners of astrology, alchemy, and the ancient occult arts were not sophisticated experimentalists, but many of them were sincere in their search for truth and were open to criticism. However, most of the people whom we label pseudoscientists today are no longer searching. Their belief systems are frozen and no longer open to change.

"In Plato's time, astrology was an exciting conjecture about personality types and their role in society. But in our time at best it is a folk game that people use to make cocktail conversation, and at worst? Well, at worst it is a stagnant dogma—one that could even be dangerous if people were to really base their lives on it."

Frazier waited to make sure she had finished and then rose to dismiss the class. "You have your assignment for next time. I'm sure we all appreciate . . ." But the notebooks were all closed and the seats were already banging.

Embarrassed to be left standing at the lectern, Tretona gathered up her notes and headed out the front exit. Well, that was over. Now maybe she could get back to writing that damn overdue book review. A whiff of benzene in the corridor reminded her of long hours she had spent as a graduate student in chemistry. Ah well, better to be slaving over a manuscript than a chromatographic titration. But what was that other smell? Must be an aromatic hydrocarbon, but she couldn't quite place it. The fragrance intensified as the student caught up with her.

"Hey, I thought you were going to talk about witchcraft. Dr. Frazier said you would."

"Well, at the end I kind of ran out of time. And frankly I don't really have as good a feel for witchcraft as I do for the other pseudosciences. At least I *think* I have a little bit of a feel for them."

"Oh, you do. I thought it was wonderful when you read out that alchemical spell about the green lion rising up to devour the red dog. I'm sure it will work."

Tretona laughed. "Well, only if you use the right quantities of copper chloride and . . ."

"I'm sure witchcraft is a pseudoscience, too."

"Well, inasmuch as witches are self-identified. Of course, a lot of it is just plain old persecution. . . ." Tretona stopped, unsure of where the conversation was headed. "But why do *you* think its a pseudoscience?"

The woman's face was solemn, bounded by long dark hair. "Because we never deal with criticism—we never accept criticism from either outsiders or insiders. We always practice support for each other. That's what makes us so powerful."

"Oh," said Tretona. They arrived simultaneously at the heavy outside door. Tretona reached for the crash bar, thought about going first, but then pushed it open and savored the passage of hair, shawl, and even stronger patchouli.

"Yes, we've turned science on its head," said the woman. "Instead of criticizing we give support. Instead of analyzing, we nurture. In place of organized skepticism, we have loyalty and faith."

"Oh," said Tretona. "Well, of course, science isn't really intended to be the only . . ."

"Would you like to come to a Sister Celebration?" The woman had stopped by the stone wall outside Lindley Hall and was looking at her intently.

"Oh, well," said Tretona. "I mean yes."

The woman smiled—slowly—and her whole body seemed to expand and radiate warmth. "I will contact you." And then she took the path leading to Woodruff Annex.

Tretona headed back toward her office and then turned, realizing she didn't know the student's name, but the woman had disappeared.

The semester churned on. Tretona managed to come up with a bon mot with which to end her book review—"And so we see that according to Feyerabend metaphysics is the manure that fertilizes the growth of science." She finally talked the poor student who always interrupted her Honors Seminar with dumb questions into dropping the course, so those sessions became much more enjoyable. Perhaps as a reward for lecturing to his class, Frazier gave her a light committee assignment. The dogs seemed to have declared a truce with the neighbor lady who kept calling the pound.

Everything was going so well that Tretona almost wondered out loud to Helen if that witchy student had cast a good luck spell for her, but she let it go.

It was high time for the Gay Studies steering committee to regroup, so Robert Farrington invited them to his place for cocktails. "Last weekend before I close the pool." Tretona hoped it wouldn't turn into an orgy with faggots lounging all over the diving board in silk Jockey shorts. As it turned out, they might as well have been wearing mortarboards; everyone was being so frightfully academic. Robert tried to set a warm tone by kissing everybody as they arrived, and as co-chair and the only woman present, she smiled until her face hurt. But she needn't have worried (or hoped?)—disciplinary loyalties are twice as important as sexual preference.

"I do hope we aren't going to have any of those dreadful objective tests," whined Donald Mercer from the Classics department. "I couldn't bear to see Plato's concept of *eros* mangled into a multiple-choice format."

"Robert and I had discussed the possibility of forgoing exams completely," said Tretona. "We thought perhaps a term paper would be more appropriate."

"Oh, how dreary," said the new guy from Comp. Lit. His voice was mid-Atlantic, with beautiful intonation. "I can't think of anything more boring than reading dozens of pathetic little coming-out stories."

"We don't anticipate this turning into group therapy," asserted Robert. He was a quantitative sociologist and was reputed to be a very high-powered researcher. "The whole point is to show that there is a respectable body of research—here I include humanistic studies, of course—which is both intellectually and, we hope, politically liberating."

"I, for one, was not apprised of your *political* intentions," sniffed Charles, the medieval historian who was supposed to lecture on homosexuality and canon law.

"But surely by the very nature of the subject it has to have political implications," Tretona replied. "I mean in the good sense—you know, as in *polis.*" She looked to Donald for help but he was inspecting the hors d'oeuvres.

"I think we should strive for a holistic approach," said Bernie Friedman. He was a great chunky bear of a man and when he said "holistic" his whole chest vibrated like Pavarotti's. "We must remember students are *people.*" (Tretona noticed that Robert had picked this moment to refill the martini pitcher.) "People with hopes. Yes, Charles, political hopes, and anxieties and a thirst for knowledge, but also a yearning for self-approbation and self-love." (The ice grinder whirred away in the kitchen as if to inject a little cold, brittle rigor into the discussion.) "And as members of a despised minority—one which is often even nameless—they will be particularly fragmented. We must help them heal themselves, not insist on sterile academic distinctions."

A general hubbub ensued, but eventually Maurice got the floor. He was a painter, complete with beret, and as he spoke he sculpted the air over the coffee table with eloquent gestures. "Bernie's right. I say: Fuck the Administration, Fuck the Curriculum Committee, Fuck the Experimental Course Division. The whole lot of them are homophobic—you all know that. I see this course as the first shot in a whole string of happenings that will zap this campus, blow their liberal covers, expose their homophobia once and for all. I think we ought to let it all hang out."

"You can let *yours* hang out, Maurice," said Robert, "but I think they'll just cut it off. I'm keeping *mine* tucked in." It was an auspicious moment for Robert to dole out seconds on martinis and for everyone else to admire the fit of his trousers. Tretona half-wondered if he was wearing a codpiece.

Tretona tried to get things back on track. "I think the students may feel a need to deal with personal issues or at least express feelings that stem from personal concerns, but maybe we could have informal get-togethers afterwards—go off to Bear's Backroom."

"Not with minors," snapped Robert.

Bernie took everyone off the hook. "On second thought, the atmosphere in a T-group or a C-R group is so different from that of a classroom that it's probably impossible to integrate them—it would probably just confuse the students."

Everyone was so relieved at Bernie's backing-off that the rest of the compromises came easier—one essay exam at mid-semester, term paper topics to be chosen in consultation with at least one of the instructors, extra discussion periods scheduled after the lectures, etc.

Tretona stayed on after everyone had left, obstensibly to help Robert straighten up.

"Lord Mary—what a bunch of prima donnas," said Robert, sinking into an enormous velvety chair and lighting up a Benson and Hedges.

"Is that Bernie in Psychology?" asked Tretona.

"Heavens, no. Counseling and Guidance. He thinks of himself as the Ur-Teddy Bear. No claws and a bow tie."

"He had a point, though. I think students will be expecting to—well, talk about being gay, what it's like in the dorms and stuff."

"You never can tell," said Robert. "They may be pretty keen to retain their anonymity. And, of course, they won't all be gay. I think we'll get some interns from the Human Growth Center—maybe a couple of graduate students studying deviance—who knows, maybe even some CIA agents! I'm more worried about the faculty exposing themselves."

"You mean Maurice? Oh, he'll calm down."

"No, I'm worried about prissy old Donald or Charles having extra little informal tutorials with some yummy blond Adonis to count iambic pentameters or conjugate verbs or something. That's one reason I was so opposed to having the class meet at night—and Bear's Backroom, my God!"

"Oh, I'm sorry," said Tretona. "I never thought about

. . . But these guys teach male students all the time. Surely that's not really a problem."

"Well, generally you don't know who's who—you can only guess and guessing is risky. But in a Gay Studies course—my God, the mind boggles."

Robert twirled his tall-stemmed glass but his movements were so studied as he set it down that Tretona decided he must be getting a little tiddly.

"Yes, those undergraduates can be absolutely mind-boggling. The things they think of, even during lectures." And Robert launched into a long tale involving a guy who had been in his Soc 101 class and then had called him up five years later.

"It was the most amazing thing. It was five-thirty on a Friday afternoon—Homecoming weekend—when the phone rang. 'Dr. Farrington, you probably won't remember me, but . . .' We chatted a little bit and then the first thing I knew he had invited himself over for a drink. Well, we spent the whole weekend together. It was fabulous. The things he did—"

"Did you recognize him when he arrived?" Tretona asked, hoping to keep the conversation on a more restrained level.

"Heavens, no—though I don't know how I could have missed him. He said he always sat clear in the back. And you know what he'd do while I pontificated on and on about stratification theory and functional analysis?"

Tretona obligingly shook her head no.

"I'll tell you what he did. He fantasized about all the things he'd like to *do* to me. And so when he came over, he did them, a whole semester's worth packed into one weekend. I've never had such an intense, prolonged . . ." Robert sighed, overcome by the memory.

"You still see him?"

Robert resumed his normal brisk manner. "Justin? Oh, no. He lives up in Fort Wayne, I guess. Hello, I'd better let Miss Mimi in." As Robert opened the screen, the Italian greyhound whimpered excitedly and then bounded straight over the back of the couch to greet Tretona.

"What a cute little dog," Tretona said.

"Oh, Miss Mimi's a sweetheart. We've been together thirteen years now, haven't we, hon!"

When Tretona left, Robert was sitting on the eggshell couch finishing off the martinis, surrounded by exquisite potted plants, the dog's head resting on his leg.

* * *

Tretona set off on foot to the Sister Celebration. It might be better *not* to have the car along—then she wouldn't have to decide whether she wanted to take Jennifer home or not. Jennifer Abrams, the friendly student-witch, had phoned with rather obscure directions on how to get there. So here she was, decked out in a long, loose Mexican shirt (it was the closest her wardrobe came to gypsy-chic), shivering a little in the late October evening, reading street numbers on a little back street just off the courthouse square.

111½ West Temperance—there was the sign to the Windfall Dance Studio, as promised. And sure enough there were the stairs leading up and a mailbox (would Helen insist on "personbox"?) with a large moon on it.

Would there be a black cat? Incense? What if they served some kind of weird brew? Should she drink it, or plead an allergy? Should she sit by Jennifer or try to blend into the woodwork?

The apartment door was marked with an even bigger moon which was surrounded with stars made out of little women's symbols, the tails serving as twinkles. The door stood ajar. Low voices, warm laughter, and soft light spilled out into the hall. Tretona took a breath and slithered in.

"Welcome," said the woman sitting closest to the door. She gracefully got to her feet and slowly embraced Tretona, pressing her cheek against Tretona's, first the right and then the left. Tretona, taken aback, responded with the kiss-your-Aunt-Nellie stance she had learned as a child, head forward, butt back, so there was no chance of full body contact. The woman deftly slid around so that their sides were touching and wrapped her arm around Tretona's waist. "Tretona," she said, "I am Marion. I am the Maid this evening. Come meet Mother."

They approached a middle-aged woman who seemed to be sitting on a hassock. A long heavy velvety skirt surrounded her like a collapsed tent.

"Welcome, Sister," she said. "I have a bad back, would you please . . . ?"

Her escort dropped to her knees; Tretona compromised by bending down to touch cheeks, right then left. She squatted as Mother continued.

"This is the Maid—and these are the rest of your Sisters. While you are here, you will think only loving thoughts. Will you join the Circle?"

Tretona nodded. (The door is open, I can always leave.)

"Kneel please." The woman produced a small dish from under the edge of her skirt.

"Great Goddess, purify this sister of all negative elements and fill her with Sisterly Love."

"Blessed Be," intoned the assemblage. Tretona felt a cool finger rub oil on her forehead. Mother kissed her full-lipped on the mouth and then droned,

"You may now join the Circle of Love. Sisters, receive your Sister."

Not quite knowing how to negotiate her way to the perimeter, Tretona Groucho-walked over to where Jennifer was sitting and plunked down.

"Glad you made it," said Jennifer and presented her cheek. By this time Tretona was getting the hang of it and slid her face very slowly alongside Jennifer's and managed to brush an ear with her lips.

Their eyes met at disconcertingly short range as they reversed cheeks. "Wouldn't have missed it for the world," whispered Tretona to the other ear.

"Isn't the Mother wonderful?" Jennifer was watching the ritual greeting and love cleansing of some new arrivals.

"I rather fancy Maid Marion myself." Tretona was feeling

giggly; must be a post-adrenaline letdown. "Sorry, I'm kidding. Yes, I agree. She's great, very solid-looking, confidence-inspiring. How long has she been—well, in charge?"

"Oh, just this evening. Each time there's a different Mother and Maid. You'll see, we'll consult the cards later to see who's on for next time. That'll be a big celebration—harvest moon festival."

"Don't let me get involved in the draw, Jennifer. It'd be just my luck to . . ."

"Oh, the cards would never choose you so soon."

"Well, I know it's a long shot, but still, just in case—"

"Tretona, the cards *know*. If they *do* choose you, it's some special plan they have and you *must* accept, we can't break the chain." Jennifer was very serious.

"OK, don't worry." Tretona looked around the room, trying to estimate the probability of getting roped in. So far there were twelve in the circle. Of course, it depended on whether the lots were cast independently or in tandem—for a moment, she couldn't remember the formulae—oh hell, forget it.

Mother began to chant and the circle joined in:

> "We are come from the
> Goddess—
> And to Her we will return."

It was in the same mode as a Gregorian chant—even the voices could have been those of choirboys.

There were poems and more songs. The Mother walked around the circle one way with oil, the other with salt. When they got to meditation, everyone was supposed to think of someone who had done good things for them and then decorate a flower in her name and hang it on the Loving Tree. The Maid produced construction paper, scissors, glue, Magic Markers. Tretona felt giggly again but everyone immediately fell to work. When someone finished she made a little speech. "This flower is for my earth mother who bore me and nurtured me, and sends money whenever my work-study runs out."

Tretona racked her brain for a suitable flower candidate. There was Helen, of course, but she didn't want to complicate the picture for Jennifer. Finally, she picked Schulamith Elkana, "the woman who introduced me to the love of my life . . . philosophy." Jennifer beamed as she glued the lavender tulip near the top of the cardboard tree.

The celebration climaxed with the sharing of bread and wine. It was like an echo from a thousand childhood communions: "Take, eat. Take, drink." But these sacraments came from the Goddess, through Mother, and on around the Circle. It was Jennifer who tore off a chunk of bread and fed her Sister with tender, slim fingers. And it was Tretona who got the wine first as it came counterclockwise around the Circle and held it oh so carefully for Jennifer to drink. Love was streaming everywhere.

By the time they crossed their arms and held tightly to their neighbors' hands Tretona was spellbound. "Now each of you picture someone who needs love," said the Mother. "Together we will focus our collective positive energies and beam all this surplus love out to those who need it most."

Tretona thought first of Helen, but couldn't picture her. Jennifer's presence was searing her hand. Then suddenly she saw Robert as clear as could be, sitting on the couch with a martini glass. So she beamed best wishes to him—and Ms. Mimi.

* * *

The drying leaves rustled like long taffeta skirts as they walked home through the West Campus. An owl queried their right to intrude and cheeky moonbeams bounced off the paving stones around the old Wishing Well. Without speaking they paused. Tretona dropped a pebble. "Any other town but Booneville and it'd be too dangerous to walk out here at night."

Jennifer let the sound ebb away completely before answering. "You hang out with those lesbian separatists mostly, don't you?"

Tretona nodded. "Yeah. Quite a bit. Why?"

"Because you sounded like them just now—focusing on the negative, concentrating on evil."

"Well, sometimes reality *is* pretty negative—but in a way I was saying something positive about Booneville. But don't witches fight bad guys and stuff like that?"

"The separatists criticize the evil in men, even their symbol is the Amazon axe. Witches exalt the love in women. Our sign is Diana, the Moon."

Tretona sought a Libran compromise. "I guess both can be valuable."

Jennifer was firm. "The best way to destroy evil is to ignore it, put all your energy to positive uses, strengthening yourself and others."

"So why do you bother about putting down separatists?"

Jennifer's black hair flashed in the moonlight. "I'm not criticizing, I'm just observing."

Tretona gave her a little hug. "And a good observer you are, too. You're right, a little analysis of patriarchy can go an awfully long way. Let's not talk about that. Can you identify mushrooms? I know a path off from the reservoir where there are scads of them."

They started off again. Tretona couldn't decide whether Jennifer had a destination in mind or not. The breeze was getting colder, and she clenched her jaw to keep from shivering.

"You cold?"

Tretona nodded. "A little."

"Well, come over to my place and I'll brew up some hot cocoa."

Sounds innocent enough. No fenugreek tea or madeira madness?

"And I've even got some leftover zucchini bread."

"Wonderful, that nibble of bread and wine sort of whetted my appetite."

Jennifer giggled and turned to face her. "You liked the condiments of love?"

Tretona blushed. "It was pretty interesting how the ritual

combined elements from different religions—the chant, the communion, the testimony service . . ."

Jennifer fired back corrections. "Matriarchal religions came first. Those Christian sects borrowed from *us,* not vice versa. Their cults are derivative, not ours. Witchcraft is the oldest of all religions. It degenerated during the Middle Ages, of course, because of the persecution from the Catholic Church and later from the Puritans. Today we are regaining it in its original pure form, with all its original power to transcend the natural order and transform lives." They arrived at narrow wooden stairs leading up past a screened-in porch to a second-story apartment. It was unlocked (were keys too negative?) and Jennifer pushed open the door. Tretona paused at the doorsill, letting her senses sort out the stimuli: smells of patchouli; herbs drying in baskets hanging from the ceiling, which was painted a plum-lavender shade, decorated with silver stars and an upside-down model of Neuschwanstein; windchimes and a mobile of polished wishbones over a maple rocking chair (smell of oiled wood?); Turkish prayer rug facing a stone altar with lavender candles and a gorgeous Japanese enamel box; Indian duri as bedspread, pillows with crocheted covers, one a pinkish plum, one burgundy.

Jennifer switched on the tape deck. "Well, come on in. Thought you were cold."

It was either the bed (too intimate) or a rocking chair (too distant). Tretona settled on the floor, sitting back on her heels, elbow propped on the bed. It was firm and smelled of lavender. She kept looking around for a cat or a pet (familiar?).

"Could you give me a photograph of yourself, just for a couple of minutes?"

"Why?" Tretona shuffled through her wallet and finally picked out the ID picture on her British Museum Reading Room card.

"I want to introduce you to Ishtar—she's the Good Spirit of this house." And without further ado the ID card was placed face down on top of a little glass case on the altar. It had a little clay head inside.

After a minute, Jennifer said, "The birth date's wrong on this ID."

"No, it's not," said Tretona, glancing at it before putting it away.

"Well, there has to be a mistake *somewhere,*" said Jennifer confidently. "I wonder if you could be adopted or something like that."

"What are you talking about?" said Tretona. "You think I don't know my own birthday? If you ever met my mom you'd know I was no orphan—we're like two peas."

"Well, I can't explain how the mix-up occurred," insisted Jennifer, "but I *know* you're not a water sign. I'd bet anything."

"Oh, so this is all a bunch of astrology hocus-pocus." (Fat lot of good my lecture on pseudoscience did, Tretona thought.)

"Call it what you like, but I'm a Sagittarian and I've never met a Cancer yet whom I got along with."

"You call this getting along? Hey, what do you mean, Cancer? I was born on the seventh of October—that's Libra. Even *I* know that much astrology."

"But your card says July tenth. That's why I said it was wrong."

Tretona was fumbling in her wallet. "Oh, it's a *British* card —seven-ten-thirty-five. They put the day before the month—the seventh day of the tenth month!"

Jennifer hugged her so hard that Tretona nearly lost her balance. "See, silly, I was right."

"You're silly to believe all that astrology stuff."

"Oooh—what about the evidence I just provided? Girl scientist won't believe her own eyes."

"Com'on—I probably even said in class that I was a Libra."

"No you didn't. I just knew."

And then their tongues continued the duel but silently thrusting deeper and faster until the sighs came and their breasts intermeshed and then knees. The Paisley skirt came up and then Tretona's blue-jeaned thigh was massaging and lifting the soft mound. Hands full of buttocks—how convenient to find no underpants—now insert a finger on top of the jeans. Jennifer arched her back, sought the contact and rode and moaned. Her hair flew back—like on a broomstick, Tretona thought as she circled Jennifer's neck with her left arm and rolled over on top of her.

"Wait," moaned Jennifer, sitting up and stripping off Tretona's shirt. "Denim hurts." Like magic the blue jeans vanished. Renewed, intensified contact—one finger in Jennifer's mouth, the other in her vagina until Jennifer grabbed Tretona's waist and twisted her around. Then a moment's lull as they locked like figures on a Tarot card, Mouth to mouth, mouth to Mouth. Explore with nose and tongue to find the magic spot and then worry it and caress it and nip it and build it up and try to concentrate because someone is sucking you up and into them —oh my God—don't forget to keep the tongue going—oh—I can't—I can't take it—and like a double thunderclap the thumbs' St. Vitus dance—together, no longer knowing which is my feeling and which is yours flowing into me from you around through me. Molten gold, like Li'l Black Sambo's melted tigers, like base metal transmuted in the fiery crucible, like freckled ivory arms and Diana's full-moon buttocks, wispy black hair clouds.

They lay cheek to cheek. Tretona turned a little to touch tongue to lips, Jennifer sprang to her feet. (Why do people always spoil the intermission by smoking cigarettes?) Jennifer toured the apartment, opening drawers and thumping things about.

"What's wrong? What are you looking for?" Tretona hated abrupt terminations.

"I'm turning silver—it'll just take a minute."

"You're *what?*"

"Turning over all the silver in the house. You carrying any quarters or dimes? Whenever I begin a new project I always turn the silver—it's more propitious that way."

"Am I the new project?"

Jennifer didn't answer. Instead she gently turned Tretona over, face down, and laid some kind of furry stole across her neck and muffled up her ears. Cool moist fingers traced designs on Tretona's back, hot cold burn tingled as the vapor trails dried. Was it Icy Hot? Now Tretona could feel the glowing on her back as Jennifer traced and retraced. Was it a moon and a cross—or maybe? Oh, of course, it was a woman's symbol.

Jennifer seemed to be dipping her fingers into something. Now along the breasts' contours, reaching underneath her, circling the nipples, but never touching them—please touch soon —no burns—what if it were acid? Tretona thinking of tensing but the rhythm so soothing, so persistent—a trail of dry ice dry fire—ovals followed by push-pulls. Wonder if it will wash off, thought Tretona. Benzene absorbed through the skin causes birth defects. What if I glow in the dark?

"I'm anointing you for the Goddess," said Jennifer in a husky voice. "I'm putting Diana's signature on your body to protect you from all evil, from all negativity."

Tretona felt guilt over worrying about benzene. Then both hands between her legs each tracing half the great circle around the pubic mound, now together up the great divide. Clitoris quivering, uncertain how to respond to the astringent visitors, then warming to the spicy fingers, awaiting their return, opening to the Goddess signs, burn me, cool me, anoint me, and as Tretona was ready to cry with wanting, Jennifer covering her, filling her, thumb and fingers, covering, filling, pulling, stroking, sweet sour crazy prickles, juicy starbursts, and still the symbols burned.

Time passed, sphincters exhausted, her back aching from arching and straining and still her flesh cried out for contact.

"Maybe we should stop," moaned Tretona.

"No, no, the Goddess wants to give you more love—much more love." Jennifer's voice seemed far away. "Much more love than you've ever known. More love than you've ever dreamed of."

The Goddess marks all over her body burnt in response and suddenly Jennifer was all over her, lips and tongue crazy, everything moving and caressing, fingers and thighs and arms dancing from moon circle to moon circle. Tretona's body tensed, as astral clouds swirled down into the center and then exploded like a supernova.

Spent, wrapped in a plush robe, Tretona sat dazed in the rocker. Jennifer massaged her feet. Slowly she came back to herself. I have to lecture tomorrow morning, she thought. Wanly, she dressed, said goodbye and started for home.

Cold air and the fluorescent street lights on Atwater snapped her awake. Once out of Jennifer's force field, her thoughts switched to Helen and as she neared home her guilt and confusion grew.

What the hell was she doing? OK, she didn't feel so close to Helen anymore but shouldn't she analyze the situation, work out what was going on, before setting off on a witch hunt?

Not that she was committed to Helen. After all, it was Helen who was always putting down monogamy. Still, Helen wasn't playing around—at least not as far as she knew. Besides, what Helen believed in wasn't the point, was it? How about her own values? What did *she* believe in?

On the other hand, what harm had been done? Jennifer obviously had enjoyed herself. No trust with Helen had been violated. Or had it? Could there be a one-way contract? And what about herself? It had certainly been exciting. But God, I could never have any sort of serious relationship with Jennifer —turning silver, household gods, what a weirdo.

Yet all that warm sister love mush stuff was kind of nice. Is there really anything wrong with indiscriminate unqualified love? Even if it was only skin deep and only lasted through one séance, surely that was better than sessions full of analytical hatred of the patriarchy. But are those my only choices?

As Tretona turned off Atwater and into her drive, anxiety was choking her. She'd have to talk to Helen—no way around that—but what could she say? Sleepy dogs jumped to attention as she slipped in the back door. Shushing them, she switched on the dining-room light. There, propped against the soy sauce bottle, was a note in Helen's neat hand. "Hi, hon. How was the coven? Think I'm coming down with something, so I've hot toddied myself off to bed early. The dogs need walking. H."

More miserable than ever, Tretona wrapped some bologna around a carrot and followed the dogs around the block. Their boundless energy made her feel a little better. Maybe she should think twice before talking to Helen. No sense in hurting her unnecessarily.

That strategy buoyed her up for half a block, but as she turned south into the path of a nearly full moon it hit her that Teresa had probably rationalized her own deception the very same way.

Well, at least it didn't have to be tonight. Helen was fast asleep.

10.

Analysis—and Synthesis

An Airedale bopped by with kangaroo bounces, carrying a briefcase in its front paws.

"What's your hurry?" asked Tretona. She seemed to be sitting between the roots of an enormous oak tree.

The Airedale paused, breathless, and spoke with an accent like Darwin Frazier's.

"I must deliver a very important dossier. It's terribly urgent, you know."

"What dossier is that?" asked Tretona in a tiny Alice voice.

"Here, see for yourself," said the Airedale and dumped the contents of the bulging briefcase on a picnic table. "Oh, dear. 'Love,' 'Tenure,' 'Community.' I'm afraid the folders are all scrambled."

"Maybe I can help," said Alice.

"I'm afraid you'll have to sort it out entirely. I'm busy." And the Airedale galloped away unencumbered.

A gypsy wagon pulled up. It had a Periodic Table painted on the side and kerosene lamps mounted on each side of the driver's seat. Wonder Woman appeared from inside wearing a skin-tight lavender jumpsuit and silver cowboy boots. Her hair was in a bun and she was frowning.

"Why are you wasting time?" she demanded.

Tretona hesitated. "Because I can't find what I want, I guess."

An Amazon swung down from the oak tree brandishing an

axe. "Be strong. Join the Revolution." She slapped the side of her leather shorts impatiently.

A gypsy in black lace came from behind the wagon. "The Goddess is Love—come to her now." Her arm grew longer and longer, stretching toward Tretona.

"What shall I do?" Tretona asked Wonder Woman.

"Look in your heart," came the reply.

And when Tretona looked down her heart was glittering like a disco bauble, flashing out beautiful colored beams as it turned.

"My heart is of many colors," said Tretona.

"Look more closely," said Wonder Woman.

And when Tretona bent down she found that the heart was made of a million tiny little mirrors which reflected and refracted the images of the purple jumpsuit and the Amazon's axe and the gypsy sequins.

"It has no light of its own," cried Tretona. "It's all made out of mirrors."

"That's only the cover, silly," said Wonder Woman. "No wonder you can't navigate. Better unwrap your heart."

So Tretona began picking off the mirrors and the Amazon disappeared and the gypsy disappeared and Bebop thumped her bed and whined for attention.

Tretona struggled awake. Christ, it was late. And she had more to do for her lecture at eleven. Quiet efficiency. Turn on the kettle before taking the dogs out. "Wait a minute. Didn't Helen walk you?" she asked. Three tails wagged yes but all the hyperactivity suggested otherwise. "You'll have to settle for the back yard," she decided.

Maybe she should skip washing—no, damn it, her skin still felt crinkly. Last night flooded over her. Christ, I've got to shower. Why hadn't Helen wakened her earlier? She knew Wednesday was her big day. Hell, Helen was probably pissed.

Quick slug of coffee, a bit of cheese shoved into pita bread, don't forget the briefcase, and Assistant Professor Getroek set off for school.

"Lots of people looking for you this morning." Was the departmental secretary taking attendance now? Don't be paranoid.

What's this in the mailbox? Tretona lifted the tissue paper and discovered an enormous daisy-shaped cookie. "Manna moon beams from the little Sisters of Diana" said the card. Tretona felt vaguely annoyed.

"Is it your birthday?" asked the secretary cheerfully.

"Er, no—just a joke," said Tretona evasively.

A green memo fell out of the tissue paper. It was from the Chairman—good thing she hadn't thrown it away by mistake.

A matter of enormous urgency has arisen. Please see me at once.
D. Frazier

Wonder what was up now with Darwin. Well, it had to wait. She had at least two references to check before eleven o'clock and she really ought to review the homework questions she'd assigned just in case some were tricky.

Actors claim that no two performances are the same. Some new nuance of interpretation is always possible, or the scenery can fall down. Teaching has even more uncertainties. The odd student question can be unnerving. "But didn't Einstein show that everything was relative?" (No.) "Why did anyone care whether the earth moved or not?" (Sheer curiosity.) "But experience proves that induction works!" (That's begging the question.)

More jarring are those moments of lucidity that strike in the middle of a familiar proof when you suddenly realize there's a fatal flaw in the whole line of argument. And then there are mind lapses.

That morning Tretona got knocked speechless in the middle of doing Galileo's *a priori* derivation of the law of the lever. Darwin knew about her and Jennifer. That had to be it. He must have seen Jennifer come in with the cookie and either she said something smart or he just guessed. Damn!

She fought to get back on track. "So, let's see . . . we have the bar suspended by strings, yes? Let's back up a little. . . ."

Finally class was over. Maybe she should look up the section in the Faculty Handbook about student-instructor relationships. Technically, Jennifer wasn't her student, of course. Did that matter? Oh, hell. Frazier had been so cool about the Gay Studies course, talked on and on about philosophers being relevant to big existential issues today. Shit, what a mess.

Darwin collared her as soon as she hit the departmental common room. "Tretona, come in here, I've got to talk to you." It took her last ounce of autonomy to delay just long enough to pour a cup of coffee. And then sheer inspiration struck again.

"Hey, want some of this cookie? It appeared mysteriously in my mailbox. I think I've got a secret fan lurking around someplace."

Darwin brushed the offering aside. "Shut the door, would you?"

For the first time in a long while Tretona was aware of the possible heterosexual significance of closed office doors.

"Won't be hot in here, will it?" she asked, stalling.

Darwin practically pushed her into a chair and closed the door.

"I don't know what to do about this unbearable situation. I certainly hope *you* can propose something."

Oh boy, here comes trouble. I wonder exactly how much he knows, and about what.

"You know the new dean is automatically freezing all faculty vacancies as they arise."

Oh, so if you fire me, you'll be short-handed. Tough shit for you, Darwin.

"Well, now he's gone one further. He's got some goddamn computer formula for distributing secretarial help and we only qualify for one. We've got to lay off the other secretary by the start of second semester. What on earth are we going to do?"

"That's awful," said Tretona with considerable relief, and then with more sincerity: "That's really awful. Fire 'em over

Christmas vacation, huh? Boy, I'd like to see the dean try to fire Kelly."

Kelly was brisk and blond and typed ninety words a minute. She had browbeaten Darwin into allowing her to work with a portable TV blaring. ("Why should you care? It increases my productivity.")

The only time Tretona had ever seen her stop and really watch it was during the investiture ceremony for Prince Charles. Kelly loved royalty.

"Kelly has seniority—it's Louise who would go."

No wonder Darwin was so shattered, Tretona thought. Louise was arguably the single most important member of the department. She could type anything—German, Latin, modal logic, tensor calculus. She advised the graduate students on everything from where to look for an apartment to which faculty members abhorred split infinitives. Louise took care of Tretona's birds while she was gone to conferences and kept Kelly from throwing away records just because they were three years old. She made coffee and kept the newspapers tidy and put philosophical jokes on the bulletin board and brought a mug rack from home so people didn't have to drink from Styrofoam cups and was nice to undergraduates and consoled faculty members who gave bum lectures or had stomach aches or car trouble or lost dogs.

"They can't make us fire Louise," Tretona said. "How can she have less seniority?"

Darwin shrugged. "She didn't start working until her husband died, or maybe they were divorced, I don't know. She's only been here four and a half years. I looked."

"*Only* four and a half years? This whole thing is so ridiculous I can't believe it."

Darwin looked mollified now that his frustration was being shared.

"You say the dean's using a formula? Well, we'll just have to challenge it, that's all. What goes into his infernal computer anyway?"

Darwin shrugged. "I don't know exactly. Number of faculty, number of student-credit hours taught, the usual stuff, I guess. He wouldn't tell me."

Tretona was out of the chair by now and pacing. "Well, here's what we do. First we get the formula. Kelly can do it. She knows all the staff over at the Computer Center and at the dean's office. Then we leak it to the student paper. It's sure to be a ridiculous formula. But first we tell Louise that no matter what happens we won't fire her. We could hire her on an hourly basis out of grant money for a while, couldn't we? Surely by that time the staff union will show a little gumption and . . ."

Darwin was beaming. "You really have a good head for practical matters, Tretona. You would make a good departmental chairman."

Chairperson, Tretona thought, but then smiled and said, "Boy, I hope we can pull it off. No wonder you looked so worried this morning."

She walked out of the cigar-and-tweed atmosphere of Frazier's office into a cloud of patchouli. Oh my God, Jennifer must have just walked by. For a moment Tretona looked forward to telling her about the morning's false alarm, then quietly reconsidered. The perfume trail led straight to the Ladies'. But Tretona suddenly turned on her heel, whispered to Louise, "I've left for the day—ten minutes ago," and slipped out the side door. A little detour through Morrison Hall put her closer to the woods and from there she had a clean getaway.

Boy, do I need to sort out my life, she thought. All of a sudden, the huge campus seemed potentially swarming with people she didn't want to see. Where to hole up? Jennifer was at the office; Helen might be back at the house; the Daily Grind wouldn't do—too many folks she knew went there. Oh hell, try upstairs at Rapp's. Only lone undergraduates or winos hung out there in the daytime.

She tried to sort things out as she walked. What did she want anyway? Someone who shares my basic beliefs. Some*one* or some*ones?* Well, both really. God, you're fussy and what are those basic beliefs anyway?

Well, that's harder to say, but I can't stand people who have lousy epistemologies. Worse than bad breath? No, I'm serious, they can't be anti-science and they can't argue *ad hominem* against every idea that might have been originated or endorsed by a man.

Ad hominem? Pretty cute, but what about love and understanding and warmies? I want some of that too, please. And intelligence and humor and—hell, Tretona, you don't just want a friend, you're looking for a veritable paragon. (Paragona? Paragirl?)

Am I being utopian? It's true no one is going to exemplify every star-struck virtue you've got in mind. Still, I'm really not going anywhere with Helen and her gang. I should cut loose. "Never let go of nurse—for fear of finding something worse." Jennifer would be worse, that's for sure. But more exciting.

Tretona's Libra brain continued to juggle alternatives as she crossed Dunn Meadow and might have remained forever in a state of dialectical equilibrium if Fate had not intervened.

Little wispy beard, tall slumped shoulders, feet on the verge of duck walking, it couldn't be, could it? Searching eye contact—

"Alan!"

"Tretona! By God, I knew I'd find you!"

"Alan Bruck, what on earth!"

Hugs and pokes and nine—no *ten* years of catching up. I can't believe it, Tretona, you really left chemistry? And *you* don't play the violin at all anymore? Alan, child prodigy with the magic bow and the Paganini fingers and the incipient stomach ulcer at age fourteen—now, laid back and playing jazz piano with a group on tour.

"I would never have expected to find you in Booneville, Indiana, Tretona. But then I saw your name on this Gay Studies poster."

"Oh, where?" (Robert was obviously on the ball.)

"Down next to the Bluebird. That's where our gig is. You gonna come hear us?"

"Sure thing. Alan, this is so great. Let's go get a sandwich.

No, let me buy you lunch. You like quiche? We could go to the Godlen Horn or—what do you like these days?

Alan's eyes sparkled. "Tretona, could we possibly go over to your place and make something? We're on the road so much, eating out all the time, I just got this terrible yen for Kraft dinner mixed with Campbell's tomato soup. . . . You remember how we used to . . ."

"And butterscotch pudding afterward? Alan, you haven't changed a bit. Remember when I lived in the basement over on Green Street?"

"Yeah, and we used to have to wash the dishes in the shower because the sink was plugged up?"

And so they giggled and reminisced and it was only as they crossed Atwater that Tretona remembered her agreement with Helen not to bring boys into the house without prior consultation. Hell, maybe she wouldn't be there. Oh Christ, there was her pickup.

"Alan, we'll have to go to the grocery. Wait in the car and I'll see if my roommate wants anything."

Not auspicious. First witches, now boys. Helen, sorry not to give advance notice but old college buddy—

—But I haven't seen him for ten years!

—Helen, he's got an ulcer and I *promised* him home cooking.

—Well, I guess then *you'll* have to leave. I'm sorry, but it *is* my place.

And that's the 51st way to leave your lover.

11.

Lavender Window in an Ivory Tower

The students shuffled in. Yes, this is 209 Morrison Hall. Maybe we better wait a few minutes, it's a little hard to find. Robert was pacing around nervously. Besides, queers are always late, thought Tretona. She and the other auxiliary instructors sat up in front unaccustomed to the cramped chair desks, not quite knowing what to do with their briefcases.

"It's almost twenty to eight. I think we'd better start," said Robert and his co-instructors all nodded encouragingly.

"This is E333: Perspectives on Homosexuality," said Robert authoritatively. "My name is Robert Farrington. I'm from the Sociology Department. As you know, this is an experimental course and we are going to approach the topic of homosexuality using a multidisciplinary approach. Before I introduce my colleagues, I'd like to summarize the requirements for the course."

He outlined items on the blackboard and the students dutifully scribbled them down. Does the term paper have to be a research paper?

No, but it must conform to the standards laid down by the instructor to whom you submit it.

Drone, drone.

Now the instructors were introduced. At last a chance to turn around and see who had showed up. Tretona didn't recognize anybody. Which closet had these kids crawled out of? Maybe they were all just psych majors.

"According to the computer list, twenty-nine students

signed up, but I don't think that all of you are here," said Robert. "Why don't we just go around the room and people introduce themselves, say which year you're in and your major—if you've chosen one."

"Do you think we could put the chairs in more of a circle?" The questioner wore a red T-shirt that said "Come out—come out" and was carrying a book called *Riverfinger Woman*.

They all obligingly shuffled their chairs around, smiling a little now. Tretona ended up between a chunky little guy with pimples who looked about seventeen and a very tall blond woman who was wearing mascara—she *had* to be a spy from the Administration, or at least bisexual.

Their majors made sense for the most part—Counseling, Psych, Music, Anthropology. Two women from Forensics also were wearing makeup. The tall blond glass-of-water was doing an M.S. in social work. There was one other graduate student, a sort of rumpled, bearded guy with a pipe. "My name's Paul and I'm doing a doctorate in math," he announced, "but I'm here because I write pornography."

Tretona wondered what Robert would do. He was staring at his syllabus and seemed not to have heard.

"Gay porn?" she asked.

"Oh, of course," came the reply. "The *Blue Boy* book of the month club has published several."

Now the students plunged in. How'd you get started? How long does it take you? Do you use a pseudonym? Does it pay well?

Robert gaveled for order with his note pad. "We will have a discussion of gay literary themes later from Dr. Wardley, correct? But this evening we need to start with some basic etymology and definitions and Professor Mercer is going to do that for us. Donald, it's all yours."

Donald immediately started scribbling Greek words on the board—*agape, eros, storgeiludus*. Popular interpretations of Plato and Mary Renault notwithstanding, it would appear that the Greeks actually sanctioned only a few forms of male-male in-

teractions—however, certain scenes on Greek vases do seem to
indicate that at least in imagination—

How irrelevant it all sounded. Just another complicated,
scholarly puzzle, like whether Aristotelian prime matter possessed the potential to become hot/cold, wet/dry before acted
on by form.

—the clearest examples involve older men, wise teachers, in
an extended pedagogical relationship with special pupils, those
with the most promise, one presumes—

Had Mercer intended a tiny joke? No, probably not, he was
footnoting himself again. "As I suggested in a review of Dover's
book . . . extended pedagogical relationship . . ." She thought of
the scoutmaster who had recently hanged himself in the Booneville county jail before coming to trial on charges of molesting
a Cub Scout. A married man, a fine record of community service.
What would the Greeks call his behavior—teaching, playing,
uncontrolled animal lust? Or would the Greeks even have had
a word for the strange contorted ferment of emotions that must
have been at work, which led the poor man from Sunday School
class to that pup tent beside a campfire to asphyxiation from his
own long-sleeved shirt in a 6-by-8-foot cell. "It was a polyester
blend," said the sheriff. "Cotton shirts won't knot up that
tight."

Mercer had somehow jumped to the nineteenth century.
"And so I think we may safely conjecture that the first recorded
case of Lesbianism occurred in 1869."

What on earth was he talking about? The women in the
class were looking disgusted. Hell, why hadn't she paid attention!

"Could you possibly expand on that a little?" Tretona
asked diplomatically.

Donald seemed pleased at the interruption. "It is surprising,
isn't it? You see it was in 1869 that a German physician treated
a woman who ran a girls' boarding school. She had become
dysfunctional and been committed to an insane asylum. After
extensive interviews he diagnosed her as suffering from a new

disorder, what he called *die konträre Sexualempfindung*. Italian researchers translated the term as *amore invertito*, which led directly, of course, to Havelock Ellis' concept of the *invert.*"

Tretona was impatient.

"So what you want to say is that Lesbianism was first classified as a *disease* in 1869. That, of course, has nothing whatsoever to do with its existence."

"Can we really say that something exists in a culture if that culture has no name for it?" Donald's Socratic tone was dripping with smugness.

"We sure can," said Tretona. "If we have two women who are sexually-romantically involved, we have lesbians as far as I'm concerned. What about Sappho?"

"Ah! I was coming to that. Let me summarize the entry in the Oxford English Dictionary for you. *Sapphic* refers only to a complicated verse meter until 1890 just as *Lesbian* refers only to a mason's ruler until 1908. I repeat, Lesbianism does not exist until the last half of the nineteenth century."

"By that logic," Tretona replied haughtily, "there was no gravitational attraction before Newton, no oxygen before Lavoisier, and no natural selection before Darwin. You gotta distinguish reality from concepts."

"Oh, indeed," warbled the lecturer. "But when self-conscious human behavior is concerned, concepts are largely constitutive of reality."

"I agree it makes a difference when we give a phenomenon a name." Tretona was fighting to stay calm. "But look at the names people picked—Sapphism, Lesbianism. They went right back to the Greek stories that had been there all along. So they had the *concept* of women-sexually-loving-women all along, even if they didn't have a simple word for it."

Robert was becoming nervous. "I'm sorry to say that our time is up and I did promise to be punctual about bringing official proceedings to a halt. Perhaps as an exercise, the women students could look for earlier instances of Lesbianism. It does look difficult if there's no word. . . ."

Tretona blurted out, "And perhaps, as an exercise, the men students could look for earlier instances of rimming and Frenching. Since the Greeks didn't have a word for it I suppose that it didn't exist."

"Uh, hum." Robert was determined to conclude on a positive note. "Well, yes. And do read the assigned chapters in Tripp and the articles on Reserve in the library. See you Thursday!"

Tretona was immediately besieged by the women students. What was all of that about? Is he trying to take our history away from us? The Greeks didn't have a single word for men either so why does he say that's so different? How can he say lesbians didn't exist? What about women in harems? Yeah, and in India where even the wives have girlfriends, too.

Tretona realized she had to calm things down. "Look, we've got lots of time to sort all of these things out. There is *something* to what he said. How you define an activity or define yourself is important. He's too much of a cultural idealist for my taste, but that's one of the things that makes team teaching exciting. Look, we'll hash it out next time."

The group dispersed, mumbling: What's a cultural idealist? I don't know. Were the Amazons lesbians? I've got a book of Greek myths—we can look. What about Ruth and Naomi?

Tretona eased back toward Robert and the rest of the faculty. Better end on a friendly note.

"Well, you got us off to an exciting start, Donald," she said cheerfully.

Mercer looked grateful. "I'm glad you think so. I'm afraid I might have confused everybody." He stacked his notecards neatly, produced a rubber band for them from his vest pocket, and filed them away in an enormous briefcase.

The minimal niceties completed, Tretona headed for home. The January night was cold, damp. Why couldn't Booneville be in the snow belt? This must be the only place in the world where you could get mildew and frostbite simultaneously.

She shouldn't have reacted so violently to old Mercer. Now all the women in the class would get their paranoid hackles up and there was really no need to. Premarital tension, that's what she had. Every day since Helen had moved out she had told herself how much better it was not to be in a situation where her principles were compromised, how she would never make new friends as long as Helen was there, how important it was to develop the resources to live alone, how it was a time of growth. And every day when late afternoon rolled around she knew she ought to call someone up and make a date for supper or coffee or a movie, and sometimes she even did it, and other times she built a fire for herself and the dogs and made popcorn and waited for the news to come on and made a rule not to eat until after the news unless she had someplace to go that evening and every bedtime no matter how wonderful the day had been if there's no one to share it with—on all of these occasions Tretona knew that she was lonely, so lonely that her muscles lost their timbre and her brain flailed around like an exhausted swimmer.

Was it prudence or fear that enabled her to ignore Jennifer's little messages? Or was it simply the fact that Jennifer had no phone and hence was out of immediate range when the ache was worst?

And why hadn't she at least advertised for a roommate when second semester began? Was she too proud to admit that she couldn't live alone, or afraid that she'd end up trying to seduce whoever moved in?

It wasn't as bad as after Teresa left, though, in a way, *she* really had left Helen. Maybe it was just humanly impossible ever to hurt that much again, the nerve ends must get numb after a while.

And what good was a Gay Studies course for dealing with what people really worried about? All the history and literature and political theory in the world couldn't touch that terrible feeling of being alone, of being so separate and different from everyone else, of hating the clear cold panes that keep us all apart. Yet the awesome gamble of daring to rupture them, bursting through like Evel Knievel, never being sure of the reception when we actually touch other flesh, and hoping, trying, fabricating a fusion until we split back into two and get resealed in glass cages and this time the walls are even more transparent, but twice as thick.

"Professor Getroek! Can we ask you something?" A group of women emerged from Bear's vestibule. They looked like they were from the class.

"We're just going into Mother Bear's for a post-mortem. Will you join us?"

Just what Robert had feared—fraternizing (sororitizing?) with the students.

"Sure," she said.

When they reached a booth, there was a bit of shuffling around. They suggested Tretona go in first but some residual mixture of claustrophobia plus butches-don't-sit-on-the-inside flared up.

"Why don't I fetch a chair?" she said. "Since there's five of us."

There was an awkward silence when she returned. Miss Come-out T-shirt broke it. "Want a menu?"

Tretona took charge. "I don't remember your names at all. I'm Tretona."

Beth, Lisa, Becky, Julia came the response. Tretona repeated the listing hoping she could remember it. "Well, Beth-Lisa-Becky and Julia, what shall we order?"

"Beer!"

Good, they weren't under-age—or else they were enterprising enough to get fake IDs.

"Professor Getroek—"

"Tretona, if you don't mind."

"OK. I'd like to ask you a question."

"Sure, if I know the answer—shoot."

"Did you have any trouble in your department getting to teach a Gay Studies course?"

So Tretona told Frazier's story about wanting to make philosophy relevant. "I think he was also hoping that there'd be hundreds of people taking it. He's always worried about class enrollments. Actually, I'm surprised we got as many as we did. Did you have any worries or hassle about siging up?"

Beth had just told her advisor she was going to take an elective but hadn't decided which. "He'll find out when my mid-semester grades come in." Lisa was taking every deviance course in the catalogue anyway Julia needed credit in an advanced Arts-and-Humanities to fulfill distribution requirements.

"Are you sure it counts?" said Tretona. "I'm not sure whether experimental courses qualify."

"No, it counts. I checked with the dean's office."

The pitcher of beer came.

"It really is going to be pretty experimental," said Tretona. "Not so much because of the subject matter, but because of the team-teaching. Believe me, trying to coordinate nine faculty members—"

"What was that turkey going on about tonight?"

"I'm afraid my mind wandered just at the crucial step," said Tretona, "but I think this was what he was trying to say. When people do something—like drinking beer, say—they don't just go through the motions, like say a worm would. Do worms drink? Well anyway, people think about what they're doing and it takes on a social meaning. Like when I drink beer with you, it's not just because I'm thirsty; it's because we're—well, having a friendly glass of beer. So the way we think about activities becomes an important part of the activity itself. And since we think in words—at least we have to use words if we're going to communicate what we think—if you look at the concepts available in a culture, it gives you a pretty good clue as to how those people are thinking about things, and since how you think about it is part of the meaning of what you do, if there's no *word* for lesbian, then in that sense there are no lesbians."

"But that's just bullshit," said Becky, bold as her T-shirt.

"Well, a lot of the concern in the women's movement about language—Ms., chairperson, stuff like that—is based on the same premise: social reality is in part constituted by language."

"Well, I think feminists are bull-shitting themselves, too, if they think pronouns are going to make any real difference. Laws, votes, money, power—that's what counts." Tretona noticed how strong Becky's hands were.

"I want to get back to lesbians and forming concepts," said Julia.

"You can make the concepts, honey. I'll take lesbians any day." Beth was getting silly.

"Oh, shut up. What I think is this: people don't need words to feel things. Like I bet a lot of kids masturbate for a long time before they know the word for it."

"Ha! Now it's out, Jule. I always knew your sexual repertoire was bigger than your vocabulary."

"Stop acting like a dumb dormie, Beth." Julia pursued her argument doggedly. "And anyway people make up words for things. What was that private word in *Patience and Sarah*, Lisa? You read it out the other night."

"Melt," said Lisa and blushed.

"Yeah," said Tretona. "But a lot of times when you're growing up you think you're the only person in the world who feels that way. And even if you have a lover, you don't conceptualize it as loving women, you think of what you're feeling as loving Boobsie-Sue, and you're sure you could never feel that way toward anyone else."

"Look, I think everyone knows right away that they're queer," Becky said. "But some people are just afraid to admit it."

"But what if your society doesn't have a word for queer," said Beth. "Then there's no category even to admit to."

"Every society has a word for queer/taboo/forbidden/ no-no / unspeakable / I'll-kill-you-if-you-even-think-about-it. They have to, otherwise there'd be lesbians all over the place." Becky underlined her words with strong finger thumps.

"Well, not quite all societies," said Tretona. "We'll get some anthropological data later on in the course—"

Becky interrupted. "OK. I've figured out what's wrong

with that asshole's argument. He says no lesbians until 1869, right? Now—what happened in 1869? Somebody invented a new mental illness category. But lesbians aren't sick, so playing by his rules, there weren't any real lesbians until—name your date—maybe 1969 and Gay Liberation. And of course there weren't any gay-studies–SIU-type lesbians until right now!"

"I'll drink to that," said Beth.

"I assume you knew each other before you took this course?" Tretona said, hoping to quell the clashing of glasses.

"Mercy, Maude, yes. We're Exhibit Q-3 at Foster Quad. We all live on the same floor. Everyone's pretty nice to us except when their folks are visiting. Then they start looking the other way in the corridors and the parents stare coldly." Julia continued. "We all have single rooms and try to be fairly discreet except when Becky comes over wearing her outrageous T-shirts and spouting politics in the lounge."

"How'd you meet Becky?" Tretona was surprised at her own curiosity.

"In the weight room—where else?" Beth chorused.

Becky looked a little embarrassed. "I'm a percussionist and so I need to keep in shape. I don't know what these other yahoos go over there for."

"To check out women with beautiful bods who are wearing Rubyfruit T-shirts," Beth answered.

"Can you imagine," said Julia. "The first time we got up courage to go into the weight room with all those sweaty jocks, who should we see but ole Becky doing bench presses and wearing this lavender T-shirt with *Rubyfruit* sprawled all over her pecs."

"I told her she ought to put *Jungle* on the front of her sweatpants," said Lisa, and blushed back into silence.

What a difference a few years can make, thought Tretona. It was painful just to remember her own undergraduate days in the fifties: closeted, the occasional secret chat with the only two other lesbians on campus as far as she could tell, bedroom door closed, low tones, their eyes haunted and faces drawn.

Now look at these kids in the seventies, bopping around in the dorms wearing bumper stickers and lavender beanies, teasing and joking and taking a Gay Studies course in their spare time.

And yet the binding horizon of fear was still there, a little further in the background perhaps, but still there, lurking, flavoring every day's activities with a paranoia. Hadn't they worried about her security as a teacher? And they obviously realized all too well that some parents down for Homecoming weekend might file a complaint, insist that their darling daughters be moved to a decent, healthy corridor. What if they got a homophobic residence assistant who would hound them over minor rule violations? What recourse would they have? And suddenly the gaiety and hyper-energy of her four students reminded Tretona of the forced cheeriness of a party awaiting a hurricane. There's no use posting a guard and there's no use being afraid. Disasters strike randomly. It'll either come or it won't. Even Becky's T-shirts became a sort of daredevil stunt, brave but terribly risky. I dare you to beat me up, ostracize me, call my mom, give me a C, she seemed to be saying.

"So you must have quite an interesting wardrobe, Becky." Tretona got back into the conversation.

"Well, everyone is always saying we ought to get more political, so this is my little contribution. It's really *very* interesting wearing these shirts. Lots of people stare, but not a single person has made a hostile remark. One guy in the weight room asked me if I picked pink grapefruit and I said, no, that was the name of a lesbian novel and he said, 'Oh, that's pretty intense,' and went on with his forward curls."

Becky continued, "I reckon most people don't get it and those that do mostly don't care and those who do object—well, it's a funny thing. If you carried a picket sign or posted something on your dorm door, you might get some flack. But T-shirts are different, it's become acceptable to wear really strange T-shirts. So I don't think it's such a big deal—at least not on campus. I'd think twice about wearing one down to the Farm Bureau Co-op."

"You'd probably wear your Peterbilt baseball hat down there, wouldn't you, Becky, huh?" Beth was giggling.

All the hijinks buoyed up Tretona's spirits, but by the time she reached home she was lonelier than ever. Those undergraduates were the most positive women she had met since London. Yet she couldn't quite imagine herself hanging around the weight room.

Bebop woofed apprehensively as she opened the door and then jumped up, paws on shoulders in ritual greeting. Little Seker wiggled around her feet.

"Down, guys," Tretona gasped, but already she was falling and as she grabbed for the coat rack her right hand raked along the wall and an enormous splinter lodged under her fingernail.

Tretona sat among the frightened dogs and dislodged jackets and bawled, the deep, noisy sobs of a child who is tired and hurt. Finally she went upstairs to get a needle. As she sat on the bed under Zelda's watchful eye and tried to pick the splinter out using her clumsy left hand, certain things became crystal clear. There's not much I can do about finding the right lover. There may not even be much I can do about finding really close friends. But I sure as hell can find someone to pick out splinters and stop the hollow echoes in an empty house, someone to give me a reason to wash the dishes before I leave in the morning, and someone to take the occasional phone message and commiserate with me about Booneville's wretched winter weather.

Don't dump all your needs in one basket, she thought. Let's try parceling them out.

12.

A Pilgrim from Moldavia

When in doubt, let fate decide. And so Tretona, dubious of the wisdom of taking in boarders, especially while temporarily cheered by the unusually bright winter sun, put up one very discreet notice in the vestibule of Mother Bear's:

Room, share kitchen.
Would suit quiet dissertation student
Must love animals.

Two days passed and then she got a call from a graduate student in anthropology. He sounded nice enough over the phone but said something crazy about being tired of camping out in his van.

Tretona sat at the dining room table waiting for him to arrive. What should she do about the gay issue? It seemed wiser to make sure he knew, yet wouldn't it look defensive to bring it up? Maybe she should have borrowed a Rubyfruit T-shirt from Becky. Still, there was a Lesbian Concentrate sticker on the mirror in the bathroom and a big poster celebrating Fifty Years of the Lesbian Novel at the top of the stairs. That would have to do.

An ancient VW van drove slowly by the house, hesitated, and then backed expertly into the driveway. One taillight was dangling by a bare wire. The battle-scarred bumper sported a fluorescent sticker, Nuke the Whales.

As she watched, the driver rolled down the window, reached down for the door handle, let himself out, and then rolled the window back up before slamming the door. The rusty fender skirts flapped in the winter wind.

The prospective roomer was short, stocky, and wearing a sheepherder's jacket. Tretona quickly put the dogs in the basement and opened the door. His eyes were black almonds, amazingly intense, amplified by extremely long lashes.

"You've come to look at the room? Come on in. No, your shoes are OK." Actually, they were awful, relics from Napoleon's invasion of Russia.

The visitor unbuttoned his coat and shook out a thick braided pigtail that fell halfway down his back. He wore one heavy gold earring.

"My name's Zabro." His voice was low-pitched and extremely resonant. "I'd shake hands but they're a mess."

There were open cracks and red splotches all over them and the knuckles were swollen.

"I guess they got chapped or frostbitten or something. I've been camping out in the bus and it was fine until that cold spell hit right after New Year's."

Tretona decided to ignore that topic of conversation—hell, she wasn't running a flophouse—and conducted the tour of the house as planned. Keep TV turned down after eleven, bottom shelf in fridge is free and this part of the cupboard.

"Oh, I don't cook."

Here's the bedroom. Could manage an extra bookcase if you need it. Ironing board in hall closet. That's Zelda there on the curtain rod. She likes to sun in your room but will leave on request.

"Everything looks fine."

Back down to the dining room table. Tretona, unsure of whether to continue to play the role of prospective landlady or start in on will we be friends, offered tea.

"I've got stuff in the van," said Zabro and reappeared with a six-pack of Buckhorn beer and a brand-new checkbook.

Tretona read the inscription:

> Cuza Zabroscu,
> Yellowwood Campground
> Booneville, IN

"You really were planning on camping out all winter?" she asked.

"Yeah, I wanted to get in shape for an assault on Mount McKinley next spring, but I think I'm just getting run down."

"What kind of a name is Zabroscu?"

"Gypsy—mostly Rumanian, I guess."

There was something about his demeanor that discouraged Tretona from following up on any of the fascinating leads.

"My name's kind of unusual too—Getroek."

"Yeah, I know. You're teaching that Gay Studies course."

Jeez, everybody in town must have seen that poster. Tretona assumed the rather forced, cheery, open manner that she adopted when discussing sensitive issues with straights.

"Yes, it's going very well. An intensive introduction to gay history and gay culture, all in fifteen weeks."

"One of the things I'm going to force myself to do while I'm in Booneville is get to know the gay community," said Zabro.

Tretona was cautious. "Sort of an ethnographic exercise?" she said lightly.

Zabro's eyes went opaque. "No, it's much more personal," he said and crushed his empty beer can.

Christ, thought Tretona. Is this guy a closet case or a psychotic homophobe?

"Well, I really don't know all that much about it," she said carefully.

Zabro stared at her intently, then shrugged and opened another beer.

"Now London is a different matter. Everyone's so relaxed and friendly. And so many gay guys in England are quite stylish.

When I left the clone look hadn't hit there yet. They all looked like fair-haired, pink-cheeked, carefree schoolboys."

Zabro coughed and his lungs rattled like dry gourds.

"Not all schoolboys are carefree," he said and went off on another bronchial binge.

"Are you feeling OK?" said Tretona.

"No. Look, I want to stay here, but right now I'm sick and I know I'm a little crazy, and I won't cause you any trouble, but I thought it was only fair to tell you." Zabro clenched his beer and a new crack appeared across one knuckle.

Tretona's mind raced; what on earth was she getting into? Should she ask for references, or—? Bebop started barking and crashing against the basement door.

"I better go let the dogs up."

The doggie triumvirate streaked through the kitchen and surrounded Zabro, sniffing gingerly at his shoes and then growling from a safe distance.

"Peace," said Zabro and extended his weather-cracked hand palm down. Within two minutes Bebop had her head on his knee for intense ear scratching, Pearl was wagging her tail nonstop, and Şeker was lying under his chair. Within three minutes Tretona had accepted a check for the first month's rent.

* * *

Some people make you a present of their life's story, neatly packaged and tied with a bow. Others dole it out in stingy little bits, tiny jigsaw pieces which mean little out of context—dry anecdotes that only pretend to further intimacy. Zabro's revelations were like the souvenirs in an adventurer's attic—rich, exotic, abandoned, and in wild disarray.

He seemed to have grown up in Montana, but had detasseled corn in Iowa, worked on a whaling boat, played the cello well enough to be in master classes, and studied logic, Greek, and auto mechanics before turning to anthropology. Zabro's father seemed to be a gypsy alcoholic lawyer, who loved baseball, wore three-piece suits except for one Halloween when he got drunk and streaked after some trick-or-treaters in his

Adam-in-the-garden outfit. He also beat both Zabro and his mom. Tretona couldn't figure out how often or how hard.

Zabro admired his father intensely, hated him to the point of murder fantasies, and once admitted that he would give anything in the world to make his father approve of him.

"That's why I'm studying anthropology," he said. "My father is terrified that I will go native permanently."

Tretona had given up trying to unscramble Zabro's "gypsy logic," as he called it. She had also given up trying to figure out how his metabolism worked. He appeared to be living on a daily diet of one twelve-pack of Little Kings, starting at four P.M., with one can of V-8 juice and two Stresstabs in the morning. He never acted drunk and he never seemed to be hung over. However, his hands shook badly and he looked much older than his tattered passport said he was (twenty-three).

Their lives quickly sorted out into a pleasant, stable pattern. Zabro slept late mornings, which left Tretona free to pad about disheveled and grumpy until the coffee took effect. He took over supervision of the dogs' midnight ramble so Tretona didn't have to bundle up after an evening's body toast in front of the fireplace. He politely disappeared when she got a phone call or had papers to grade but joined her in sneering at "M*A*S*H" and pounding on the floor when the basketball team fucked up. And they had great conversations on every topic imaginable—except the gay community.

Tretona couldn't even diagnose his sexual preference. Zabro was equally oblivious to SIU's blond seven-foot center and the stunning ebony cheerleader. Tretona's faintly lascivious remark about Hawkeye Alda and Hotlips Swit ("They're almost yummy enough to make you consider swinging with heterosexuals") was met with a noncommittal chuckle. Zabro was openly affectionate with Bebop and terribly nice to the paper boy (who screwed up their delivery about twice a week and had to be phoned). That was it.

Tretona even dropped a hint about inviting Robert over one night while she was doing a post-mortem on the Gay Studies class (someone had brought up S-M and everyone had got all agitated), but Zabro squashed that with an "I'm sure you must have lots of business to discuss."

"No, I thought maybe you'd like to meet him. He's a very nice, a very interesting guy."

Zabro just shrugged. She did wangle out one bit of information one night when she was drunk and complaining about Valentine's Day coming and here she was with no lover. "Don't you ever get lonely, Zabro?" she babbled and then stopped, embarrassed that he might think she was coming on to him.

"I've been celibate for five years," he said quietly.

"Twenty-two, twenty-one, twenty, nineteen, eighteen," she said, counting backward on her fingers. "Eighteen? Christ, you were just a boy!"

"No, I wasn't, that was the trouble," he said and went out barefoot in the cold to fetch in more firewood.

It was Bebop who finally got the story out. Tretona was grading papers in the dining room late one afternoon. She heard Bebop come down from upstairs, jump up on the couch and start chomping on something, but she didn't really pay any attention. There were bones and chewtoys secreted all over the house.

Zabro came in, said hi and went on into the living room. "Oh no!" he groaned.

Tretona leapt up and found Zabro on his knees rocking back and forth in agony. "It's my monkey paw," he said, and showed Tretona the remains of a shriveled little hand.

"Bebop, bad girl!" said Tretona. "I'm awfully sorry. Can we get another one someplace? Was it special?"

"You stupid woman! Of course it was special. Do you think I'd bawl over any old monkey paw?" Zabro was bent double, his head hitting the floor.

"Zabro! Stop it! What on earth is wrong?"

And then she got him to hold his head up and finally he sobbed, "Ted gave it to me. Uncle Teddy gave it to me. It was the only thing I had left."

And then Zabro got up and calmed down immediately and

brought in whiskey and ice and told the story in a dry, abbreviated fashion as if he were reading out a police report. How he had met Edward Selkin when he was fifteen. Fell in love. Idyllic stolen rendezvous for three years. Planned to move in as soon as he graduated from high school. Father found out, destroyed Ted's picture and everything. Ran away to Ted, who promptly said Zabro wasn't a boy any longer and so he couldn't love him. And that was it.

Tretona was puzzled. "What'd he mean you weren't a boy? He was older than you were, I assume. You just now called him Uncle Ted, didn't you?"

Zabro laughed bitterly. "God, yes, he was older. I never knew for sure how old, Grecian Gold and all that. He must have had fake ID; his driver's license made him out to be thirty-seven, but sometimes things he said about pop tunes and movies from when he was in high school just didn't add up."

"So why did he mind your advanced age? Jeez, you weren't over the hill at eighteen, were you?" Looking at Zabro's dissolute condition now, Tretona suddenly wasn't sure.

"Hell, no. I had just started lifting weights and was really fit and filling out. That's when I blew it. He was a chicken queen, Tretona."

"Oh, surely that's just an excuse. You must have grown apart, or he found somebody else, or was getting bored, or maybe something else was changing in his life."

Zabro's face hung like a gray death mask. Finally, he sighed. "That's what I kept thinking, but it doesn't check out. I finally talked to some of Ted's friends a couple of years later and they said it was a set pattern. They were surprised it lasted as long as—" Zabro's voice was gravelly.

"Then why in the hell didn't he warn you?" Tretona's memories of her own betrayal fueled her anger.

"I guess he thought it would be different this time. Maybe I *was* a little special to him, or maybe he always thought it would be different. I don't know, Tretona. I've thought about it, believe me, I have. For five years I've replayed everything we ever said to each other, everything we ever did. I loved him so much. You can't imagine. I just can't understand what went wrong." Zabro's hands and jaw were tight.

Tretona ransacked her brains for some way to cheer him up.

"Where does old Edward live, Montana? I tell you what we'll do. Let's load up your van with sleeping bags and trail mix, we can take the dogs, too. Then we'll go on a cross-country vendetta. First, we'll go find Teresa—I think she followed her little fiddle player off to Texas or something—and throw cow manure all over her front porch, and then we'll bop up to Butte or Bismarck or wherever the hell it is and kidnap old Edward and take him to a deserted cabin and give him nothing to eat but Colonel Sanders' Kentucky Fried (until he's sick of chicken) and we won't let him out until he promises to wear a badge that says 'I like older men' for a year."

Zabro managed a wispy smile. "Actually, I don't hate Ted. He gave me an awful lot. If it weren't for him, I might never have found out I was gay, you know. Or it would have taken me a lot longer."

Tretona's Pollyanna detector flashed on, so she decided to change the subject. "So, tell me about the monkey paw."

For once Zabro was generous with details. On a hike with the Outbacks—about ten of them—he'd seen Uncle Ted around—knew he was a good mountaineer—the group wasted a lot of time looking at a bear through binoculars—didn't look like they were going to make it all the way up to the lake— Zabro disappointed, hoping to photograph some nesting loons —Ted volunteered to go on ahead with him double-time—so they huffed and sweated up the trail—clouds came down, then cold drizzle.

"We'd better take shelter," said Ted. "You're a skinny kid, gotta watch out for hypothermia."

"Shit, man. I can make it."

Actually, I was scraping the bottom of my lungs, said Zabro. Ted was in a lot better shape than I was. Besides, he had on a poncho.

"There's a ranger cabin coming up. We can wait out the storm there."

My teeth were chattering. I couldn't even put on my sweatshirt 'cause it was wrapped around the camera.

There was a sign on the cabin door: No entry without permit.

"Hey, man. We can't go in there."

"Well," said Uncle Ted, "if they come to arrest us, maybe we can borrow a jacket for you." He pushed open the door, got a fire going in no time, made me take off my wet things, and wrapped me in a blanket. The wind screamed like a siren and I couldn't stop shivering.

"There should be an emergency cache of food around here. Let's raid the pantry."

Ted rummaged around in a firmly latched cupboard. "Damnation," he said.

"Have the rats eaten it all?"

"No, goddamn trespassers."

"We're trespassers."

Ted ignored it.

"All they've left us is a can of beans and there's no can opener."

"Don't you have a knife, Ted?" For some reason I felt scared.

"No." He sounded angry.

"Why not? I thought you were such a big outdoorsman—poncho, map, matches . . ."

I shut up—I thought he might slap me.

"If you must know, I *had* a beautiful Swiss army knife and gave it away—to a twerp no older than you. I'll be back."

And he dashed out the door. The rain sounded like shrapnel. I was too scared to move. I wondered where bears went during storms. I wondered if bears could open doors. How could I fight a bear without my jeans and boots on?

Ted reappeared, soaked up to his thighs.

"What happened to you?"

"Slipped into the stream. Got a good stone though."

As I watched he pounded one rock on another, which split, and he kept chipping away until he had a kind of a point and then he opened the beans and used the stones to make a little platform in the fire. It was beautiful to watch him.

Then he took off his pants, wrung them out and hung them by the fire. But first he smoothed the creases back in, just so. I almost said something smart, but thought better of it.

"Guess I'll have to share that blanket, Zabro. It'll help warm you up anyway. How you doing, mate?"

And then he smiled and I smiled. And pretty soon the beans were boiling. So he used his sock as a hot pad.

"What are we going to do for a fork, Ted?"

And without a word he made chopsticks out of some of the twigs in the kindling box, but I'd never used them before and I was still shivering so he fed me bites, and I was kind of embarrassed, but he just talked about how birds feed each other, not just parents and babies, but during mating rituals and sometimes just for friendship.

When the beans were all gone, I drank the leftover juice—or tried to—but a lot dribbled on my chin so Ted wiped my face with his sock and I made a smart remark about the smell and we kind of got to wrestling but then I felt his cock and quit.

I finally started to get warm—the fire was roaring and the laundry was steaming and Ted's leg was hot against mine so I kind of opened the blanket a little and Ted said maybe I should lie down and rest a while and he found me a little split log for a pillow and said the Japanese always used wooden pillows.

An then it got very quiet and Ted sort of dangled his fingers across my chest, real casually, and all of a sudden it was like my entire body got an erection—I don't know what it was—anxiety, desire, nervous exhaustion.

"Don't do that." I could hardly talk.

"Why not?"

He kept wisping his fingers along my breastbone and down around my belly button.

"I mean it, Ted. Stop. I'll get a hard on."

"Oh, we wouldn't want that to happen."

And he started playing with the hairs on my belly.

"Goddamn it, don't touch me."

My voice sounded very weak and far away.

"OK. *I* won't touch you."

And he reached over for his pack and pulled out the monkey paw. I couldn't believe it.

So then he stroked me with the monkey paw—he said the monkey's name was Jocko—and at first I giggled and then I got quiet. And Ted made me shut my eyes and told me a story about Jocko and how he loved to caress young boys and touch their skin and how he didn't like body hair very much because he was a monkey and he was hairy but boys weren't like monkeys, they were different and there was one place that was never hairy but smooth and sweet—

Tretona had had enough details. "So you got it on with a phantom monkey, huh?" she cracked.

Zabro looked a little stunned.

"I'm sorry, Zabro. Seriously, how did you feel about it? Was it a sort of a date rape—a fuck or die-of-exposure party—or what?"

Zabro paused. "I never thought of it as coercion before, although I suppose there was an element of that. Hell no, I was just a skinny horny kid whose blue jeans were always too tight in the crotch."

Silence fell in the living room. Bebop raised her head, looked around, groaned, and fell back asleep.

Zabro scratched her belly with his toes.

"Well, that's the end of Jocko," he said. "And Ted. I think I'm free."

13.

Identity Isometrics

"Hey, Zabro, *who* are you? Identify yourself in four words or less," said Tretona, throwing her briefcase on the table.

Zabro stared at his beer. "Oh, my God—girl philosopher's got brain-fever again. *Who am I?* Who wants to know?"

"The Gay Studies teacher, that's who."

"Oh. Well. In that case I'm 'The-Queen-of-Siam'—four words exactly. What on earth are you ranting about?"

"Hell, I've got an assignment to write. For my own class, can you imagine? Bernie, the world's cuddliest shrink, 'facilitated' tonight and we all have to write about our identities. It can be an essay or a poem, or anything we like. But they're all supposed to be anonymous. Isn't that weird? How can you have an anonymous identity? What on earth shall I write? What would you say, about yourself?"

Zabro began dictating. "I am my penis. I stand straight and tall. Sometimes I shoot off my mouth unexpectedly—"

"Zabro, stop it! Jeez, for someone who's supposed to be celibate you sure have a one-track mind."

"Sorry. It's just that ever since I got that monkey off my back, or maybe it's all the hot baths I get here."

He certainly did look a lot better. Even his hands had healed, thanks to Tretona's prescription of Cornhusker's Lotion followed by Clinique moisturizer. Zabro had changed. Sometimes he was almost unrecognizable—his hair was styled, the beard trimmed, new shoes. In a way, he was a good example of

what Bernie had been saying about how few things about ourselves are fixed.

"Actually, the session was pretty interesting. Bernie started
out by making us list five ways we were the same now as we
were when we were kids. You want to play? List five things."

"I hate shrinky head-trips," grumbled Zabro. "Just tell me
what you said."

"As a matter of fact, he called on me. So I read out the least
personal item on my list—'love Kraft dinner.' "

Zabro chuckled. "That's obviously a major part of your
identity. What'd he say?"

"Well, it was kind of funny. He just asked me to name ten
foods that wouldn't be on the list. So I did—carrots, cottage
cheese, olives, shrimp—you know how picky you are as a kid."

Zabro reflected a minute. "Then there are all those horrible
kiddy treats you wouldn't be caught dead touching now—Kool-
Aid powder, Jell-o, Twinkies, Sugar Pops. Makes me sick to
think about all the garbage I used to eat."

"Exactly. So Bernie made the point that people sometimes
think that their identity is some hard-core thing down inside
that never changes, but that couldn't be right because surely the
changes in my favorite foods were just as significant or maybe
even more so than the overlaps. Then he made a little sermon
about how we can choose what kind of person we want to be
and—"

Zabro was playing an imaginary gypsy violin.

Tretona laughed. "That's exactly the way Becky reacted.
Remember her—Ms. Rubyshirt? Anyway, she said it wasn't the
quantity of similarities and differences that counted, it was the
quality. Like I probably *adored* Kraft dinner or I wouldn't even
have said it. But the main point was that certain things out of
our past *are* fixed in us now—she wasn't arguing that they were
genetically fixed—but however we got them, we're stuck with
them now."

Zabro looked solemn. "A Kraft dinner addict for life, eh?
What a fate!"

Tretona grinned. It was wonderful to see Zabro perk up.

"So then our friendly local pornographer asked Bernie how you went about changing your identity. And Bernie said the best way to change your future was to change your past, to rewrite your own history."

"What an airhead," said Zabro. "Too bad they can't shrink their skulls to fit their brains."

"Now wait, listen. So then he got Becky to read out something on her list that she didn't approve of much. So she said she was squeamish, always had been, was always supposed to be the big tomboy but actually was too scared to touch fishing worms.

"Then Bernie said maybe we ought to make sure everyone understands what 'squeamish' meant so he called for examples. It was really weird what people came up with—won't look in the toilet before flushing, won't touch raw chicken, won't put a hand down the garbage disposal even when its turned off, won't eat tripe.

"Bernie waited until about a dozen examples had been given and then asked Becky how many applied to her. It turned out none of them did. As a matter of fact she had cleaned out an outdoor toilet site when she was eleven years old and had pulled her cat out of the corn picker and taken care of its mangled paw.

"And then Bernie said: Let us now rewrite Becky's history. As a child Becky had an extremely strong stomach that permitted her to do things that would have made others blanch. She is even more strong and sensible today."

Zabro looked thoughtful. "It all depends on where you throw the spotlight, doesn't it?"

"Exactly. Our past is fixed but we can go back over it and choose today which aspects we want to highlight and build on."

"Oh, hell." Zabro looked discouraged.

"What's wrong?" said Tretona.

"Oh, I was just about to fall for that old existential individualistic bullshit again. Look, Tretona, the self is a *social* construct. Read Margaret Mead on the Arapesh—Social Psych 201—labeling theory and symbolic interactionism. We find out who we are by looking in the mirrors that society provides. If Becky's mirrors told her she was squeamish, then she *was* squeamish, by God, and there's no use her pretending to decide she wasn't."

It was Tretona's turn to feel discouraged. "Boy, Zabro, whoever said social science was liberating has got to be crazy. You are so bogged down with cultural determinism and the hegemony of the first two years that you can't even think about radical change."

"No, I didn't say that. I just said it couldn't be unilateral. Becky just can't *decide* on her own that she's not squeamish. She might try to, but society has got to validate her new perception of herself or it won't stick."

"Zabro, you're right! I'll be goddamned. Of course, that's exactly what was going on in the class. We *all* looked at Becky's behavior and *we* all decided she wasn't squeamish, no matter what her pop said about fishing worms. You're absolutely right. Becky needed *our* reactions before *she* could stop thinking of herself as squeamish. Of course, she had to believe us. In the end, she really did have control, but is sure helped to have us there. That's great, Zabro!"

Zabro did not look particularly pleased with the twist Tretona had put on his theory.

"I hardly think a motley crew of SIU students meeting twice a week qualifies as a source of social validation." He sniffed.

Tretona was roaring ahead, oblivious of details. "And that's why you can't come out of the closet alone."

"You're right. It takes at least two to tango, darling."

"That's not the reason, silly. Since all the mirrors in the society we grew up in distort and stigmatize gays, the *only* way we can get a positive identity is by finding out how healthy gay people react to us. *That's* why the gay community is so important—not just as a place to pick up lovers or get sympathy when the straight world fucks us over, it's the gay community that permits us to construct a gay identity. That's why the second coming out is so crucial. Wowie zowie, Zabro, at this rate I'll have to take back all those nasty things I said about social science. 'Identity as a social construct'—not bad. That really explains a lot of things."

Zabro drained his bottle of beer and flipped the top from another one. "Well, I guess it explains why I'm better off living in a VW van."

Tretona stopped bubbling, her mood flattened by the weight of Zabro's depression. She wanted to grab his shoe or maybe even hug him, but they never managed to touch each other. He seemed to be coated in lead.

"Hey, the gay community's not perfect, Zabro, but it's not that bad."

"Isn't it? Who wants an identity predicated on poppers and K-Y jelly? Who wants to have their worth measured by the size of your cockring or the number of times you can come in one evening?"

"Come on, Zabro. It's not all like that."

"Of course, it's not *all* like that. If you prefer, you can build your identity around a gloryhole, or leather boots, or the fuzz on the cheek of your pubescent lover."

"Zabro, stop! That's not the whole story."

Zabro expertly lit a Lucky Strike, despite the tremor in his hands. "And the way you tell it, the womyn's community is no better—crazy witches or angry Amazons or alcoholic barflies."

For just a moment Tretona shared his despair. Hadn't she been discouraged? In fact hadn't she almost given up looking? But somehow the line of argument had gotten off track.

"Well, Zabro, I guess you've convinced me that it's not so simple. It's not like picking an identity off the rack in a ready-to-wear shop. You've got to tailor it for yourself. It must be some kind of dialectical thing where you have a vague idea of what you value and then you try to find people who pretty much share those values and then you get a more specific idea

of what you want—and you may reject some of your earlier
ideas about what you want to be. You don't just buy wholecloth
whatever the first group you run into says is important. But you
don't go off into the wilderness and decide it on your own
either."

"And you think that's what I've been doing?"

"Haven't you?"

Zabro sat completely still. Tretona suddenly realized how
rare it was to see him without either a beer or a cigarette in his
hands. They looked awkward in their emptiness. Bebop, who
always slept with her eyes half open, sensed an opportunity and
roused herself just enough to get her head on his lap.

"OK, Teach. I wasn't gonna tell you until I found out
whether I liked it, but just to get you off my back: I volunteered
to be on the program committee for the Booneville Gay Alliance
conference."

Tretona was speechless, but she grinned so hard that finally
even Zabro had to smile.

14.

Lavender Menace

No more leisurely sprawls in front of the fire, no more flipping through the *TV Guide* in hopes of finding something decent to watch, no more vague conversations about whether magic in primitive societies was a precursor to science, no more wistful remarks about how nice it would be when spring came. Spring precedes summer and on June 6 Booneville had to be ready to feed, house, workshop, and entertain hundreds of "purple people," as Zabro kept calling them.

The living room was stacked with lavender T-shirts. Just try making a logo out of "First Annual Booneville Festival for Lesbians and Gay Men." Tretona had averted one near disaster by reminding Zabro to remind the committee to order lots in super-big sizes. "Helen's really looking out for the welfare of the physically enlarged these days."

Sometimes it seemed to her that Zabro must be doing all the work. He was on the phone constantly, first cajoling and then bullying people into action. At first the Student Union tried to renege on the conference booking ("those goddamn fuckers claim we never confirmed our reservation") but Zabro found out from a sweet young guy in the Conference Bureau that the real problem was that there was a Boy Scout leaders' convention scheduled for the same weekend. He first threatened to sue and then suggested they shuffle rooms so that "the queers will all be in Ballantine Hall and the brown shirts can have Morrison. The lounge there is nicer, but what the hell."

The Womyn's Bookstore Collective petitioned for exclusive rights to sell books and records. The committee stupidly complied until Paul complained that then his books wouldn't be on sale.

"What am I going to do?" Zabro groaned. "Paul's our only local published writer, but there's no way those dykes are gonna sell *Blue Boy* pocketbooks."

That problem was solved by another disaster. Someone forgot to put "Child care provided" on the brochures, so the Collective decided to boycott instead of selling books. Zabro got the idea of buying a rubber "Child Care" stamp, but by the time the Collective cooled down, the book concession had already been opened up to include a co-ed store from Cincinnati.

Tretona was so tired of Zabro's mumbled curses against super-sensitive dykes that she was half relieved when Donald and some of his super-fastidious cohorts from Dignity started leaving petulant messages for Zabro.

"They're objecting to the Workshop on Womyn's Sensuality and Massage," Zabro sighed. "Martha wants to put in the program that it's for women only, but Donald says that's unconstitutional."

"Hell, can't you schedule a workshop for men in the next room?" asked Tretona.

"Well, Donald is also afraid that people will say we're having orgies on campus. He thinks we should be super-careful. Above reproach."

Tretona wondered if Donald was always super-discreet when he walked his handsome brown poodle around and around the block past the library parking lot late at night.

"Look, Zabro. You shouldn't have to make all the decisions. Can't you get the steering committee to take some of the flack from these prima Donalds?"

"Yeah, it's trying to get them all together. There's a meeting here tonight, you know, and none of the women can come. I was really hoping you'd sit in for once, Tretona."

"But I'm not on the committee. Besides I've got papers to grade."

"I know, Tretona, but it's really important that we have some women there."

Tretona fidgeted impatiently. People nowadays were always wanting her to sit on committees and to play oracle, to spout out *the* woman's point of view. A problem with secretaries in the department? Ask Tretona. Female graduate students defecting to other programs? Ask Tretona. Every other day there was a phone call: "We're really desperate to have a woman on the Building and Grounds Committee and someone said you'd be good." Hell, she felt like saying, is it my fault that only nine percent of the faculty is female and there aren't enough of us to go around?

Zabro interrupted her interior grumblings. "Tretona, I know it's a special favor, but *could* you come? I think Bobbie wants to do his drag act in the talent show."

"Oh my God, not Bobbie Boobs, the Epicene Queen of Booneville? Is this all Bobbie's idea?"

"No, you know Pierre is supposed to be his agent now. He wants to showcase the act, get bookings all over the country."

"But that wasn't the point of the talent show. Everybody else is an amateur, aren't they?"

"No, unfortunately. That would be a great out, but the Wicca Dance Troop puts on regular performances and Alex Trell is supposed to be cutting a record."

"Well, you've got to stop him somehow, Zabro, or the shit really will hit the fan. Doesn't the committee know how women feel about drag shows?"

Zabro shrugged. "Well, I tried to explain. . . ."

"Never mind, *I'll* tell them." This was one issue where Tretona did know the woman's point of view.

Thinking about the whole affair afterward, Tretona decided maybe she should have just thrown a tantrum right away instead of pussyfooting around with rational arguments. The topic came up with Pierre asking if it was really necessary for Bobbie to audition for the talent show. "You've all seen her— it's a marvelous act."

Tretona first remonstrated against making exceptions, but it turned out the lousy committee had already set any number of precedents.

"What's the problem, Tretona? You've seen Bobbie. It's a class act."

So Tretona brought up the theme of the conference, Gay Pride–Gay Unity, and said that she really didn't see how a female impersonator miming torch songs and doing comic routines with falsies contributed very much to raising gay consciousness.

Pierre affected a pose of wounded dignity: how hard Bobbie rehearsed, how integral a part of his gay identity it was to perform for gay men.

"And gay women?" Tretona added dryly.

One of the committee members protested that drag shows were a very old and very important part of the collective gay male experience.

"But can't you understand how uncomfortable it makes women feel? *All* of the jokes make fun of women's genitals or the way they walk or the ridiculous clothes they wear. Even the songs make women sound like silly, sentimental cows." Tretona wished there were more women on the committee.

"Oh, be a sport, Tretona," said Pierre. "Surely a big, strong dyke like you doesn't identify with the kind of character Bobbie portrays. Besides, think what it means to gay men: all our life we've been deprived of dressing up, of being pretty, of being graceful. Just because you dykes don't want to dress like women, don't try to stop us. . . ."

"Hold on right there, boy. Let's get clear on what's objectionable about drag shows. I wouldn't mind if Bobbie dressed up really trying to look feminine or pretty. But what does he do? He slathers on makeup, wears a ridiculous wig, simps along on his high heels and then falls off of them, shows his hairy legs,

crosses his eyes, throws his sandbag boobs to the audience—
look, while we're at it, why don't we have a minstrel show too
with Rastus and Liza jokes!"

"Oh come on, Tretona," whined Pierre. "Don't equate
camp with—"

"Tretona's right." Everyone turned to the doorway. Bobbie
walked in, trailing a suede jacket elegantly over his shoulder.
"I've been mocking my idols instead of really assuming the
character. Look, what if I do a Barbra Streisand? I've wanted to
for a long time but I was afraid I couldn't carry it off and so I
relied on humor, but I think I'm ready now. I'll do Barbra—and
I'll play it straight."

Everyone giggled at that except Bobbie and Tretona. Their
eyes locked. Tretona *knew* that even a sincere drag act wasn't
going to sit well with half the audience but she was out of
arguments. Finally she smiled, shrugged, and lowered her gaze.
Bobbie was scheduled for just after intermission.

*   *   *

It was a quiet invasion, gentle gay folks streaming out in all
directions from the registration desk, lining the cafeteria
(though there were maps to the better Booneville eateries),
lounging on the Union steps, paddling on the bank of the Jordan
River. Dykes in vans camped in the state forest or laid pallets
in the Unitarian Church basement. Dignity ran a housing bureau for men. Suddenly all of Booneville seemed lavender and
smiling. The badge Zabro wore, "How Dare You Presume I Am
Heterosexual?", took on new meaning.

Tretona's job was to put signs on all the doors where work-
shops were to be held, so she wandered back and forth between
Ballantine Hall and the Union admiring earrings and T-shirts
and keeping an eye out for gay celebrities. Every dyke in town
was there—but some of the combinations had been permuted.
Jenny Sue and Zak seemed to be together now, while Jennifer
looked like she didn't want to speak, but Tretona, in a fit of
ecumenical imperialism, stopped her with some redundant in-
quiry about whether the Womyn and the Arts Workshop

needed a room with a blackboard. Tretona was relieved to discover that the patchouli had lost its occult power and walked away marveling at the fickleness of physical attraction.

Her swinging-single cool vanished completely, however, when Helen came charging out of the lounge looking for an extra copy of the program.

"Tretona, could I possibly take your program? These womyn have just driven in from Iowa, they haven't time to register right now. We simply must plan our activities for the conference."

Tretona nodded dumbly and handed over the booklet. An entire semester lay between them, but every detail of Helen's face was still bonded into her memory—the dark, lashing eyes, a tiny, tiny mole near her ear, the way her lips poised between paragraphs.

Tretona searched for small talk even while remembering that Helen never wasted time. "How you like the conference, Helen? Pretty exciting, huh?"

Helen's mind had already moved down the clipboard. "You really should make sure that there is a womyn at the registration desk *all the time*. I had to wait over ten minutes for one to appear."

"Really? I can't imagine. The desk is supposed to be manned all the time, especially on the first day."

"It was manned, Tretona."

So Tretona fell into blushing confusion and by the time she thought to say that if Helen and her gang weren't too pure to work with boys there would have been more womyn volunteers, the moment was gone—and Helen with it.

Tretona was clear up on the second floor before she realized that she couldn't label rooms without a program. Goddamn that Helen. Acid-etched memories of the same old pattern: Helen would make an assertive, reasonable-sounding demand. Without thinking, Tretona would sweetly oblige, and then end up feeling screwed over.

Why couldn't they all use Helen's program? Tretona

fumed. Why couldn't they walk over to the Union and get another? Why didn't I say Hell no, get your own fucking program. (But they were guests from out of town.) Why didn't I say, I need my program to put up signs. (But I didn't think about that.) What difference does it make, I've got lots of time. But why do I always let Helen rip me off? (Because you don't expect friends to be selfish.) Maybe since we're friends I shouldn't mind. (But you do mind and you aren't really friends now.) Oh.

Whenever we get angry at old lovers it is so hard to remember that it's all *past tense,* that whatever our present relationship is to be has to be constructed, starting now with no special obligations inherited uncritically from other times. Turn in all the library books at the end of term. If you want to check some out again, OK. But you'd better explicitly fill out the card, not just assume the librarian knows your intentions.

A blast of hot June air smacked Tretona as she left the air-conditioned building. Slow down. She was determined to enjoy the conference. Not gonna get hassled over nothing. She smiled at all the beautiful lavender people. Good eye contact, no reason to de-focus, glance away. Welcome to Booneville, lovely gay people. How nice to feel in the majority.

"Hello, Tretona." A deep voice with lots of texture and harmonies. Sounded familiar. Oh, it was Jocelyn Rogers, the new woman in the Business School. Tretona had met her once or twice at the Women's Faculty Club. She fit in perfectly with Tretona's *a priori* conception of Business School types—eye makeup, Gucci bag, ultrasuede suit, casual chat about government mortgage annuities and meteoric mutual funds. Smart, though. Wellesley, Princeton, taught statistical methods.

Half resenting this intrusion from the straight academic world, Tretona turned to greet her. "Hi. Teaching summer school?"

"Are you kidding? I just got back from two weeks in Greece."

Jocelyn looked gorgeous. An embroidered peasant shirt, scoop neck framing an exquisite Mediterranean tan, more rosy

copper than cocoa brown. White painter pants, with a crease!
String sandals.

"Been reading the *Wall Street Journal* on the beach, eh?"
Tretona teased.

"Don't be nasty. Even capitalists need a vacation once in a
while. I would have stayed longer, but I just had to get back for
the conference. Isn't it exciting!"

Whoa, thought Tretona. What conference is *she* talking
about? Can't be the Boy Scouts, can it?

Jocelyn bubbled on. "I saw Leonard Matlovich over in
Dunn Meadow. I swear it was him, looked just like his picture
in *Time.* No uniform, of course. He was a bit shorter than I
expected. People always are, aren't they? He was leaning on the
bridge railing, absolutely surrounded by groupies. Is Elaine
Noble here yet? I might go group a little myself, though I suppose Rita Mae might object. Is she coming, too?"

Tretona was still speechless. *We are everywhere,* one in ten,
according to Kinsey. Since there were 134 women faculty on
campus, figure it out. But Jocelyn looked *so* straight. No matter
how many times the stereotype was shattered she always
seemed determined to glue it back together again. Tretona
managed to get back into the conversation.

"Just Elaine, I think. Did you get a bumper sticker? Are you
still registered in Massachusetts? Can you imagine being able to
go into a polling station and vote for a lesbian? One who's out?
God that would be such a gas."

And suddenly that little veil of I'm-more-professional-
than-thou stiffness that sometimes separates women faculty
was shattered and the two pre-tenured assistant professors
sauntered together down the sidewalk, jabbering away about
political campaign strategies and theories of voting behavior and
gossiping about whether Rita Mae and Elaine really lived in
adjacent townhouses and admiring the silver lambda luggage
tag that Jocelyn found in Greece and had made into a pendant.

"I put it under my blouse when I went into the department
this morning, but that's silly, isn't it? I'm just going to wear it."

"Isn't the Business School pretty conservative?"

"My dear, I'm very conservative. No, I know what you mean. Yes, I suppose they are. But they also understand about supply and demand."

"What do you mean?"

"Well, the *demand* for good people in business is very high these days, especially for women. And the *supply* is very low. If SIU doesn't want an excellent Bayesian statistician with good competence in computers, fuck them my dear. I'll kiss Booneville goodbye."

"Oh, don't do that. You've hardly had a chance to get to know us yet."

It was going to be a very productive conference.

15.

Vesuvius Was a Woman

It's amazing to watch feminists transform an ordinary classroom. The rigid Cartesian grids of desk chairs standing at attention before a phallic podium are swept into soft rounded contours that have no geometric center. The lectern is dismantled and shoved into a corner. The pristine blackboard is filled with cursive announcements: "Party tonight in Unitarian Church basement—Bring libations." "Anyone interested in natural menstruation aids see Betsie—I'm staying in the Union, Room 411." One linear configuration is tolerated: Row after row of leaflets on a table by the door advertising everything from writing collectives to raven totems.

The topic of this workshop was Feminist Sexuality and the room was packed. Tretona found a place on a window ledge on the far side. She hoped it wasn't hierarchical to sit up high, but soon the rest of the windows filled up. Jocelyn came in late, looked around, and then disappeared before Tretona could wave. She thought about running after her but the thought of negotiating the contoured audience was too daunting. And then Jocelyn reappeared carrying a chair. Tretona giggled a little to herself. No way Jocey was going to get those new painter pants smudged up. Wonder how she felt about grass stain? Better find a blanket. Vision of tartan rug, wicker picnic basket with champagne. No, better make it Asti Spumante, especially if Tretona was going to be wearing cut-offs.

The workshop began. The panelists were asymmetrically

distributed around the innermost curve of chairs. Women sitting on the floor in the middle looked around to see who was who as the introductions were made. "And the main topic we wish to explore is the holistic nature of womyn's sexuality, the connections between nursing and mothering and child care, and the sensuality of gardening and growing things in warm, moist soil, and the high we get from embracing our sisters and touching them. We feel that womyn's sexuality has been distorted and limited by the exclusive male emphasis on genital sex. We wish to reclaim our whole sensual-sexual natures. . . ."

There was a shout from the back contour. "Excuse me, Pat, but there's a man here and I'd like to ask him to leave before we begin. I'd like to ask him to leave right now."

The placid, undulating surface of the room writhed and boiled, little local turbulences as people asked each other Where? Who? and craned around to look.

Pat held up her hand for quiet and then said quietly: "Thanks, Mickey." Then in an authoritative voice: "This workshop is for womyn only. Any men should have the decency to leave right now. Where is he, Mickey?"

A black woman stood up and leaned against the literature table. "Mickey is wrong, there's no man here." Waves crashed back and forth. "I suppose Mickey is talking about Estelle. Estelle was born a man but she has chosen to be a woman. How many of us can say that? She has gone through a lot of pain and anguish and expense to become a woman. She belongs here just as much as you do, Mickey."

All eyes searched for Estelle. From her vantage point Tretona located her/him? without difficulty—a tall, broad-shouldered blonde sitting next to the black woman. The head was bowed slightly, hands folded in the lap.

Pat cleared her throat in a moderator-ish sort of way and spoke hesitantly: "Well—er—of course gender roles, gender identification processes are all part of womyn's sexuality. I suppose as we de-genitalize sex, it's only sensible to de-chromosomalize gender, if you know what I mean. I think that as we dissolve some of the artificial boundaries . . ."

"Bullshit, Pat." Mickey was still on her feet. "I'm not defining womyn in terms of their genitals, nor their chromosomes. I'm defining them in terms of their common oppression as womyn throughout history. It's that shared experience which makes us a womyn or not. I would think Roxanne of all people would understand that."

The black woman's answer was an octave lower and several decibels quieter.

"Estelle knows about oppression, too. And she has chosen to identify with womyn's struggle for freedom and fulfillment. I think we should join hands with her."

Mickey's voice was calmer now, but she gripped the chair back in front of her as if it were a railing on a storm-tossed deck. "A man is not a womyn, no matter how many hormone pills he pops, nor how many furs and feathers he puts on. Look, Roxanne, how would you feel if I plastered on stove polish, jived along snapping my fingers, and then tried to crash a Black Caucus meeting? I may be sympathetic as hell to your cause, but I'm not *black*. I can read poetry about racial discrimination; I can raise my consciousness; I can take supportive, auxiliary political action. But I can't *be* black. It's that simple."

Pat was waving for attention. "Look, our time is fleeting. There's an awfully big group here, it's hard to hear. Is there a Local Arrangements person present? I wonder if there isn't a second room we could use? Maybe spread out a little. The panel's too large anyway. . . ."

Tretona slid to the front of the window ledge and looked around to see if any other Boonevillian was going to speak. "There's a lounge right down the hall by the vending machines. I expect we could use it. I'll show you."

Like a beehive with two queens that is ready to swarm, the group buzzed and milled about. Who would leave, Mickey or Roxanne/Estelle? What would Pat do? Which group would be the more exciting to join? Only Tretona was committed to going to the new room. Jocelyn caught up with her in the hall. "Well, philosopher, what's the answer?"

"The answer to what?" Tretona was grumpy because the workshop had collapsed, or at least fissioned.

"You know. *What is woman? Ecce Virgo. Woman, know thyself!* I thought you philosophers had all that stuff clarified, concepts analyzed, distinctions neatly drawn." Jocelyn's eyes sparkled with mischief.

Tretona grunted. "Well, one thing we know for damn sure is that how you define a concept depends on what problem you are trying to solve, what theoretical context you're working in. If you're talking about who gets pregnant, then chromosomes and stuff are damned important. But if you're talking about political sensibilities, then you'd think Mickey would have more in common with Estelle than she does with Phyllis Schlafly or that *Total Woman* person. But obviously *she* doesn't feel that way."

"Who is Mickey? Do you know her?"

Tretona shook her head. "I think she's part of the group from western Michigan. They're very political up there. Run a newsletter."

"But why would anyone want to make an issue of one quiet little transsexual when there were a hundred and fifty full-fledged card-carrying dykes wanting to talk about sexuality? What's the payoff?"

Tretona was glad to take a return swipe at Jocelyn's profession. "Well, Jocey, the marketplace of ideas isn't quite as 'rational' as all those little consumer models they give you in Business School. I think Mickey was operating on principle, not out of a profit motive."

"Don't be too sure," said Jocelyn. "There's a pretty high value attached to being purer-than-thou. I betcha buck there's a little power struggle going on up in Kalamazoo—maybe over the newsletter, who knows—and I bet Mickey is on one side and Roxanne and company are on the other."

"We-ell, I don't know. You might be right, but sometimes I think that feminists have to work so hard to figure things out for themselves because we've been fed a *lot* of garbage, you know. And so you get in the habit of not believing *any* thing *any* one on the outside tells you. And you don't even trust yourself sometimes because we've been indoctrinated with self-doubts. So then you try to find some clear principles to guide you, carry you through while you're going through the process of systematic skepticism and reconstruction, until you can operate spontaneously, unselfconsciously again. But of course any set of principles is bound to be a bit simplistic."

Jocelyn snickered. "Simplistic, or retarded? You know the rant:

All men are (really) rapists.
All women are (really) lesbians.
All hierarchies are patriarchal.
Pronouns are powerful.
Political purity is more important than political progress.

Honestly, Tretona, do you call that stuff a theory? It sounds more like a litany to me—something you'd read off a stone tablet."

Tretona shrugged. "Yeah, there's a lot of true-believer energy involved. And some fanaticism. You know, I used to get really fed up with all the simple-minded political analyses of women's lot in our society and all the simplistic prescriptions for changing it. But then I started asking myself, how *do* really big social upheavals occur? I'm no student of political history, but I know with revolutions in science, lots of time the manifestos for a new world-view are really oversimplified. Old Newton writes down three laws of mechanics and postulates one force, gravity, and sets out to explain the whole damn universe with it. Hell, everybody knew (or *thought* they knew) that there had to be other forces—electrical forces, chemical forces, cohesive forces. But Newton said let's see how far we can get with purely mechanical explanations. Maybe light is just made out of little billiard balls. Maybe magnets just send out little streams of particles.

"Of course it all turned out to be too simple, but what amazing progress scientists made trying to implement the Newtonian program."

Jocey was grinning from ear to ear. "What an amazing analogy, Tretona. Let's see now, who is Betty Friedan going to be—Galileo? I see Germaine Greer as Kepler. Is that a sort of Newton-Leibniz controversy going on in the other room? But who gets to be Einstein, *that*'s what I want to know."

Tretona was getting embarrassed. "Oh shut up, Jocelyn. I just wanted to point out that sometimes strong, simple slogans are useful."

Suddenly Jocelyn got very serious. "Only as long as the people who spout them don't really believe them, Tretona. By far the most dangerous politicians are the ones who sincerely believe in party platforms and really try to implement them. True believers scare me shitless, especially when we're talking about social action."

"But what about pressure groups?"

"They provoke backlash every time."

"But look at the civil rights movement."

"Well, *look* at it . . ."

And so they amiably sparred their way all the way from Ballantine Hall to the Donut Shop, leaving Feminist Sexuality to take care of itself.

*   *   *

Conferences take on a rhythm of their own and by Saturday night everyone seemed talked out, ready to laugh and relax at what Zabro billed as "The Original Old Gay Amateur Hour." Suddenly *amateur* took on its original meaning—a Whitman poem beautifully read, a dramatic letter from a lesbian mother who had been imprisoned for "kidnapping" her own child, and ballads of shared oppression, "Get Rid of Those Closet Blues," and anthems of liberation, "Sing—If You're Glad to Be Gay".

There were two very attractive MCs—Jeannie and Joey—
sporting identical frilled lavender evening shirts with cumber-
bunds of a deep, royal purple. The woman introduced the men's
acts and vice versa. Good touch, Zabro, Tretona thought, and
wondered where the announcers came from. They almost
looked like twins.

Tretona scrunched down happily in her seat, knees propped
up on the vacant seat in front of her. What a varied array of
talent! Her favorite was the Wicca Womyn Dance Troup. They
worked on a bare stage—plain leotards, straight-on lighting—
no music except handclaps, footfalls, and chanty mouth noises
of the performers. Each dance illustrated a feminist concept:
"Our Power, Anger, Our Bodies, Sister Sharing." Tretona had
never seen movements that were at once so strong, yet so fluid
and graceful. Some of the women looked like gymnasts or athletes of some kind. But others were skinny, or chunky, or quite
ordinary looking. What was really amazing was how the chore-
ography capitalized on each performer's natural attributes.

The last number was called "Flowers for Georgia O'Keeffe"
and Tretona was really afraid they were going to end up with
some sort of insipid fluttery Swan Lake thing, but—no—there
were sturdy roses, thorny and stalwart, and substantial tiger
lilies, grinning en masse, and daisy chains and Venus flytraps.
The audience cheered itself into intermission.

Jocelyn had mumbled something about probably being late.
Tretona, not wanting to appear too anxious, hadn't really nailed
down plans for meeting her. She browsed restlessly at the book
exhibits outside Alumni Hall, trying to make small talk with
people she ran into and yet keep an eye out for Jocelyn. Most
of the women she knew seemed to be milling around in the big
vestibule talking to Helen. They appeared to be carrying rolled-
up posters. Tretona wondered if Helen was going to be in some
act during the second half and started scanning her program.

Suddenly someone hissed in her ear: "Dr. Getroek is a
dyke!" Tretona jumped two feet and Jocelyn chortled with delight.

"Scare you?" She hugged Tretona around the waist.

Tretona blushed and touched Jocey awkwardly on the shoulder. "Did you get here in time for any of the program?"

Jocelyn refused to change the subject. "Seriously, have you seen any of your students here?"

Tretona shook her head. "No—well, some of the Gay Studies students, of course. I never thought about it. How about you?"

For once, Jocelyn looked ruffled. "I didn't think I was bothered at all by—well, you know, coming out of the closet at the university. I really believe my job is very secure. My students like me, I really don't think it would make any big difference to them. Nobody's going to paint lavender swastikas on my office door. But yet when I walked down to Alumni Hall this evening —I was very late and nobody else was around—I started thinking, what if I run into my chairman or something? He's very formal and what if he says, 'Good evening, Dr. Rogers. What brings you to central campus so late this evening?'

"And I started worrying about what I would say, or do. I decided I'd probably walk right on by Alumni Hall and go clear around the Craft Shop and have to sneak back here from there. Does that mean I'm not really out?"

This time Tretona gave Jocelyn a real hug. "Hey, don't worry. The last thing gay people need is more bumps and bruises. You said you'd get here, didn't you? Of course, it'd be a bother to go in the side door, but if that's easier for you than confronting your chairman—hell, that's your decision. I still hide the whiskey when my grandma comes to visit. And for a long time I didn't tell my mother I had a ten-speed bike because my brother broke his hip on one and she's terrified of them. You have to pick your own battles, Jocey. If you can avoid a lot of hassle with a little effort, why not?"

Jocey was smiling again. "Actually, Tretona, I think most of the hassle was in my own mind," and she started waltzing along twirling her silver lambda pendant, acting out an alternative scenario. "Good evening, Professor Neville Stokes. Oh, I'm going to the Gay Amateur Hour. Better hurry if you're coming, we'll be late!"

"Hey, *we'll* be late! Come on, they're about to start." And Tretona dragged Jocelyn through the clump of women by the door up to the seats she had saved by tying them together with her book bag.

Jeannie was MC-ing the crowd into a receptive mood. "I guess we all had role models when we were kids. Remember your gym teacher? Or your camp counselor? Or maybe a character in a novel. Someone you admired so much that it made you hurt right here in your solar plexus? Don't get me wrong—I'm not talking about crushes, although sometimes it was hard to tell the difference. I'm talking about those people who were so wonderful and so special that they seemed almost like gods. I'm talking about those people that you tried to walk like, talk like, sing like, emulate in every way.

"Our next performer is Bobbie Lewis. He had a role model when he was a teenager. And tonight he's going to bring her right here for your enjoyment. Here's Bobbie Lewis coming to you as Barbra Streisand singing 'People Who Need People.' A big welcome now for Bobbie and/or Barbra!"

The audience clapped politely and then with more enthusiasm as Bobbie appeared in a spangly black cocktail dress. Bobbie smiled, waved, and silently gestured for the music to being.

"Sexist pig!"

"Drag shows insult womyn!"

"Leave our songs alone!"

Angry women were rushing down both aisles, shouting in voices that seemed unnaturally high and hollow.

"People—who need people," sang Barbra in a rich, musky voice, but Bobbie clutched the microphone, missing his cue. Someone turned off the tape. There were no stairs to the stage so there was a slight lull as some of the demonstrators ran around to the side door and others laid down their banners and hoisted themselves up by the footlights.

"God, isn't someone going to stop them?" Jocelyn's voice

rang out across the auditorium and suddenly people started to move. Jeannie and Joey got on each side of Bobbie, who was now shaking, and comforted him. Some guys at the front stood up and said Can't we discuss this rationally. Tretona jumped over the two people between her and the aisle and grabbed Helen by the arm.

"Helen, goddamn it, what do you think you're doing. You're wrong. Call it off!"

"Take your hands *off* of me!"

"Bobbie's not the enemy. What are you *doing?*"

"Tretona, let go of me. I'll sue you for assault."

"I bet you would, too." Tretona dropped her hands. "And what kind of assault are you perpetrating? All these people came to get together and celebrate and relax and try to form a community—and you're just spoiling everything. Bobbie's not the enemy, you dumb shit. You know that as well as I do. You're so damn keen on making some esoteric political point that you'd just tramp over anybody. I think you're a phony. I don't think you give a damn for anyone except yourself—not womyn, not children, nobody. I think you're a big ideological bully."

Helen swung her banner like a saber. Tretona parried it with her left arm and the soft pine cracked like a shot. Everyone was looking at them. Joey grabbed the microphone.

"We're going to have another intermission. *Please* disperse peacefully. Please go out immediately. Quietly please. Folks, we don't want to have to call the cops."

Someone turned on the Streisand track again and then quickly switched the tape to Judy Collins singing "Send in the Clowns."

16.

Dance for Survival

Whole encyclopedic essays could be written about the taxonomy and physiology of anger. The easiest kind to deal with is the pimple-sized Snapper Wort: it grows quickly, explodes with a satisfying whoosh, and heals almost before the rubbing alcohol has evaporated. To be avoided at all costs is that vicious perennial, Gut Rot: it begins life in the intestines but slowly creeps into the bone marrow and lymph glands and eventually corrodes the brain and petrifies the heart.

The most difficult to identify is Boil Weed. Superficially similar to Snapper Wort, one is often tempted to casually pop it, hoping for brilliant coruscations and immediate relief. Boil Weed explodes all right, but its excoriations blister and scourge like lava. Often the result is jagged second-degree burns, which are slow to heal and may even require skin transplants. Both the host organism and neighboring targets are vulnerable.

Tretona walked over toward Schowalter Fountain trying to analyze both her actions and her feelings. Her adrenalin level was falling; her arm throbbed where Helen had whacked her. She wasn't really sorry she had yelled at Helen, but it probably hadn't had any impact. Helen would just think she was pissed because they weren't lovers anymore. And how much *did* that have to do with it? Since when did Tretona care so much about drag shows? Still it was really rude to interrupt what other gay people had worked to put together. Mainly though, it was frustration that someone with Helen's obvious brains and organizational talent could be so wrong-headed.

How can you be so sure *she's* the one who's wrong? spoke up Tretona's ever-present dialectical guardian angel. No, Helen *was* wrong this time for sure and needed to be stopped—there was no use pretending an intellectual tolerance Tretona didn't feel.

But of course Helen and her crew *hadn't* been stopped— they had closed down the talent show, and maybe even wrecked the rest of the conference. Everyone was supposed to meet at the fountain after the show for a candle-lighting ceremony. It was the last week of June and some guy from New York was going to talk about the Spirit of Stonewall and then pass a torch around. Zabro had ordered dozens of drip-free lavender candles —praying there wouldn't be too much of a breeze. Hell, thought Tretona, who's going to be up for soft lights and words of love after the vitriol bath they'd all just been through? Besides, it was probably going to rain. There was heat lightning in the east— Jocey had gone off to roll up her car windows.

Quite a few people—mostly men—were milling around the fountain when she arrived. Zabro was pacing around between the soap box he had rigged up and the three cardboard cartons full of candles.

Tretona tried to smile but it was like being cheerful after a funeral. She put her hand on his shoulder. "What time you gonna begin, Zabro? Do I have time to go get a yogurt cone? Do you want one?"

Zabro's eyes were pleading. "Just stay here. If you don't mind. No one know's what's happening. I'm afraid everyone will wander off."

"What do you want us to do, Zab?" It was Pierre, wearing slinky Italian racing shorts and a wonderfully holey sweatshirt with the arms ripped off. "Shall I strip?"

"If you do, I'll throw pennies," joked Tretona.

"I know—let's play catch," shouted Pierre. And before

Zabro could object, he grabbed a box, waded through the spray, climbed on top of the limestone dolphin, and started throwing kisses and candles to the crowd. "Come on, baby. Light my fire," he sang. "Any old Boy Scouts out there? Anyone remember how to rub sticks together?"

The crowd cheered and began to improvise. Young men in cut-offs danced in the water brandishing Zippo lighters. Pierre greeted every overture with bumps and grinds.

"Always knew you were all wet, Pierre," shouted a woman in overalls and jumped in butt first.

Candles were lit and then doused by cascades of water as more people invaded the fountain.

"Well, you've got the crowd interested," said Tretona to Zabro, who was desperately moving the candles up onto the podium.

"Now to get their attention," groaned Zabro. Mr. Spirit of Stonewall stood forlornly by the podium, waiting to be introduced, while Zabro waved both arms at Pierre, but all in vain. Tretona found herself looking around vaguely for a trumpet or cymbal or something—and felt like such a fool that without thinking she threw back her head and let out a hog call: "WHOO-EY! Pierre, shut up and let Zabro begin."

Docile as her father's herds, Pierre slid off the dolphin and saluted the podium.

"Friends, neighbors, welcome to Booneville." Zabro's voice was a little shaky around the edges and Tretona suddenly got sympathy butterflies in her own stomach.

"As you know, Booneville is smack dab in the Hoosier Heartland and you can't get any more middle-America than that."

"Amen, brother. You can say that again," someone heckled in a friendly fashion.

Zabro grinned and his voice found a cadence. "We're here tonight in the Hoosier Heartland. And we're here tonight to tell middle America—and all America—that there are *homosexuals* in the Hoosier Heartland. There are lesbians and gay men all over

America, not just in New York, not just in San Francisco. There are homosexuals in Peoria and Dubuque and Kokomo. And tonight, ladies and gentlemen, there are homosexuals in *Booneville*. And we are many, and we are strong, and we are tired of harassment and discrimination. And tonight we are saying that we have had a belly full!"

The crowd roared its approval. Zabro paused for a moment, his hands folded quietly behind his back, but his chest was out and his eyes were crackling with excitement.

Suddenly a young man dashed through the crowd and jumped up on the small platform.

"Excuse me, please. Please excuse me, but they're arresting some of our people." His breath came in gasps. "They took Michael and Chuck and I don't know how many others."

Zabro took his arm. "Calm down now. What happened?"

"We were just dancing. We weren't causing any trouble."

"Where were you dancing?"

"I don't know—it was in some bar near campus."

The crowd milled restlessly.

"It was at the Silver Dollar, Zabro." Helen's clear voice zapped through the confusion. "They weren't technically arrested; they were given a restraining order and told not to dance anymore. Zak and Maureen got one, too."

Amateur legal experts flooded her with questions. "Are you sure it was a summons? What was the charge?"

"I don't know. All I know is the manager doesn't want any same-sex couples on the dance floor."

Shouts of burn it down/close it up/fuck the police.

Zabro held up his hand. "Anybody feel like dancing?" There was a full-bellied roar. "OK. But listen to me. I don't want any candles or messing around with fire. I don't want any shouting or shoving. We're all going to walk in there quietly. We're going to show them valid IDs and order drinks nicely. We're going to wait 'til everybody's in and *then*—we're going to give some dancing lessons."

Zabro jumped down and strode off across Dunn Meadow.

The crowd fell in behind, boisterous at first but then sobering as people discussed what was happening.

"Is the Silver Dollar a redneck bar? Are we likely to get beat up? Do you think we'll be arrested?" Several women from out of town plied Tretona with questions.

"It'll be all right, if everyone behaves," said Tretona. "It's an enormous barn of a place—lots of safe corners."

There were sporadic attempts to get a group chant going: "Hey—hey! Proud to be Gay." Someone started singing "We Shall Overcome" and valiantly stuck with it for a whole verse, but few joined in.

Tretona stopped worrying about violence and started being apprehensive that everyone would chicken out. But Zabro wouldn't, that was for sure. And Pierre wouldn't miss the excitement for anything. And nobody could scare Helen out—assuming of course that Helen approved of the whole enterprise. And what about you? she asked herself. She decided her only problem was that she was such a lousy dancer. What if they put a picture in the newspaper with her looking like some kind of Soviet statue in the middle of elfin balletomanes?

And what about Jocelyn? Would she be up for a dance-in demonstration? Tretona thought about waiting up, trying to find her, but the momentum of the crowd and her own eagerness to see what was going to happen urged her forward.

She was amazed at how mundane and matter-of-fact everyone was at the door. "Lot of you folks from out of town, eh?" The ID checker was cheery, obviously pleased to see business perking up. "Yeah, just got out of a fantastic concert," a proper-looking middle-aged man remarked. "Oh, I don't know, I thought it was a bit of a drag!" cracked his companion. "You're right, it *was* a drag," said a woman in a tank top.

Unlikely warriors, thought Tretona. How cool we all are—how adept at masking our true feelings. Of course, we've been practicing it all our lives.

"Ah now, here's a Hoosier," said the cheeky young man, glancing at her ID. "Oh gosh, you're faculty—I'm sorry."

"See, you never can tell who you're talking to," said Tretona. "We're everywhere."

Inside it was dark and cool. People standing three deep at the bar. Revolving prisms sprayed light showers against the wall. The music ebbed momentarily. "Don't forget, it's always request time at the old Silver Dollar—we play the old—we play the new—and you don't even have to bribe the D.J.—but I'm drinking Stroh's."

And as the music came up everyone came out on the dance floor, bodies swaying, faces beaming. There was Estelle, tall and willowy, with Roxanne, who was bouncing around like a super-ball. Pierre was directing the whole assemblage with his butt and Zabro seemed to be dancing to invisible gypsy violins. The Q-3's from Foster Quad were circling around Becky. Tretona hesitated. They didn't need her; this was a good time to get a drink.

"Come on, Teach!" And Jennifer pulled her out into the current. Suddenly the music percolated through Tretona's defenses.

"Go on now, go—walk out the door," she sang. Goodbye fear. Goodbye reticence.

"You're not welcome anymore." Because I have a community.

And then with one voice the dancers proclaimed their determination: "Did you think we'd crumble? Oh no . . . *we will survive!*"